PUFFIN BOOK

Skin Deep

Tony Bradman was born in London in 1954. He has written poetry, picture books and fiction for all ages, has edited many anthologies of poetry and short stories, and has also reviewed children's books for the *Daily Telegraph*. Tony has three grown-up children and two grandchildren, and still lives in London.

SKIN
deep

edited by
Tony Bradman

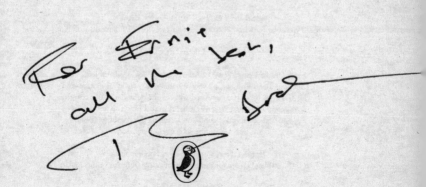

PUFFIN

PUFFIN BOOKS

Published by the Penguin Group
Penguin Books Ltd, 80 Strand, London WC2R 0RL, England
Penguin Group (USA), Inc., 375 Hudson Street, New York, New York 10014, USA
Penguin Books Australia Ltd, 250 Camberwell Road, Camberwell, Victoria 3124, Australia
Penguin Books Canada Ltd, 10 Alcorn Avenue, Toronto, Ontario, Canada M4V 3B2
Penguin Books India (P) Ltd, 11 Community Centre, Panchsheel Park, New Delhi – 110 017, India
Penguin Books (NZ) Ltd, Cnr Rosedale and Airborne Roads, Albany, Auckland, New Zealand
Penguin Books (South Africa) (Pty) Ltd, 24 Sturdee Avenue, Rosebank 2196, South Africa

Penguin Books Ltd, Registered Offices: 80 Strand, London WC2R 0RL, England

www.penguin.com

First published 2004
1

This collection © Tony Bradman, 2004
Zebra Girl © Janet McDonald, 2004
The Blokes © Alan Gibbons, 2004
The Pavee and the Buffer © Siobhan Dowd, 2004
The Domestic © Allan Baillie, 2004
The Great Satan © Farrukh Dhondy, 2004
Smoke © Sean Taylor, 2004
Assignment Day © Nick Gifford, 2004
Beads © Manjula Padmanabhan, 2004
Cousins © Merav Alazraki, 2004
Justice © Rasheda Malcolm, 2004
The Returnee © Chu-Ching Chen, 2004

Set in 12.25/14.25 pt Monotype Bembo
Typeset by Rowland Phototypesetting Ltd, Bury St Edmunds, Suffolk

Made and printed in England by Clays Ltd, St Ives plc

British Library Cataloguing in Publication Data
A CIP catalogue record for this book is available from the British Library

ISBN 0–141–31505–9

Acknowledgements

Thanks to Penny Morris, who commissioned this book in the first place, and to Francesca Dow and Rebecca McNally who actually let me do it, and to Helen Levene, an editor it's been a joy to work with – I'll miss those daily emails! Thanks also to exemplary agent Hilary Delamere, who has raised listening to this particular client to a fine art, and to the writers, of course, a world XI of the highest quality. Your patience has been much appreciated!

Contents

For Jacob O'Flynn

Introduction

The stories in this book are set in many different parts of the world – Britain, Ireland, Australia, the USA, India, Brazil, Japan – and at first glance you might wonder what they could possibly have in common. The answer is simple. Each story explores the impact on young people's lives of something that has stained human history since before records began – racism.

It's a word that has been defined many times, and one that is constantly used in private arguments and public debates, in homes and in newspapers, on the streets and on television. But for me it's always meant one thing: doing wrong to human beings because of the colour of their skin, or some other fact about their culture or background that they can't change.

I don't remember how I first became aware of racism. I'm white and English, and grew up – and still live – in London, a very multicultural place. But the rule seems to be that where cultures meet and mingle there are always tensions. So I've seen racism in all its many and poisonous forms – the ranting of racists with banners and leaflets on street corners; the hissed hatred of an old-age pensioner in a bus queue when the kids in front of her are black; the casual, shockingly racist remark made by a relative at a family party, someone you'd thought up till then was a decent human being.

At any rate, after years of seeing racism around me, I decided that I would love to put together a collection of short stories that tackled the subject head on. It seems to me that fiction is a great way to help us understand why racism happens and what it does to people. You can read any number of weighty tomes and academic text-books on the subject, but stories about living, breathing characters and their problems go straight to the heart.

You're now holding that collection in your hand. It's taken several years and a lot of hard work to bring it into being, but it's certainly been worth it for me. And whatever colour your skin is, whatever your background or beliefs, I'm sure you'll find stories and characters in these pages that will move you and make you think. Stories that will show you the differences between us are usually no more than skin deep, and often not even that.

Tony Bradman

Zebra Girl

by Janet McDonald

A story set in modern-day New York, USA

The sun draped a strip of light across the small, pale feet propped on the window sill. Dale slid her bony hips forwards on the metal chair and then backwards. A gangly twelve-year-old, she twisted her legs this way and that until they were out of the light, safe from the sun's reach. When her body was positioned just so, she held it absolutely still, aching with discomfort. Wet flakes of snow blew in on gusts, coming to rest and slowly melting on her bare feet, pyjama pants and into the woollen shawl she'd pulled, shivering, on to her chest.

On the blustery street below, a woman leaned the brim of her hat into the wind, pulling behind her a plastic-covered shopping cart filled with groceries. As she turned on to her block she raised her eyes towards the windows of her apartment building. She was on the lookout for kids armed with water balloons, eggs or tomatoes who might be lying in wait for an easy ambush and hearty laugh at the expense of their neighbours. If the parents raised their children to have some respect for grown folks and for each other . . . being poor was no excuse to treat each other any old way. Her gaze scanned the sunlit facade for sudden shifts of light. But on this bright morning the rows of windows remained still as closed eyes. She glanced up at her tenth-floor apartment and suddenly stopped. What the . . .?! The back-room window was wide open and snow was flying in like it too was fleeing the cold. There was a movement. Then feet. What was that child doing, trying to catch her death of cold? She rushed to the building, clasping a jangle of chilled keys.

Upstairs in another room, a finger with a rainbow-coloured nail traced a heart in the moisture of the windowpane. 'Nay & Ray, 2-gether 4-ever.' Nadine flopped on the bed and switched on the TV. Singing and humming along, she watched hip-hop dancers with long black weaves, red-painted lips and beige skin, slither and slide their way through music videos. A defective radiator hissed and bubbled as it overheated her room so that at that moment, in the middle of winter, the sixteen-year-old was wearing a white leotard. The bleached whiteness of her outfit contrasted starkly with the dark brown of her skin and her white headband gleamed against the cascade of curly black hair it held in place.

A key turned in the front door and Mrs Lutter burst in, stamping snow from her heavy shoes. She rolled the squeaking cart into the kitchen, its wheels tracking water on to the floor.

'Girl, what in the world are you doing back there?' she shouted down the hallway. 'Are you out of your mind?'

Two doors banged open and out ran the Lutter girls, nearly crashing into each other.

'Watch out, Zebra Girl,' snarled Nadine, giving her sister a shove. She called out, 'Nothing, Mom, just watching TV.'

'Shut up! And quit pushing, skank!' snapped Dale. 'I'm not doing nothing either, Mom!'

'I'm gonna say this one last time to the both of you. I will not tolerate name-calling in this house! Now come here, Dale!'

Nadine pointed her butt at Dale. 'Ha! I knew it was you!' She lowered her voice, 'Zeeeebraaa . . .' and sashayed back into her room. Dale kicked her sister's door and hurried to the kitchen, still barefoot and wrapped in the thin shawl.

Things weren't always so sour between the sisters. Indeed, they had begun quite sweetly. The night before her sister was to come home from the hospital, Nadine lay awake thinking. Five years old, she barely distinguished between her new sister and her old toys. She imagined the baby with eyes as large as dolls' and cheeks as fat as a teddy bear's. She felt it on her lap, warm and round. She saw them staring and smiling at each other. The baby arrived, all eyes and cheeks. And so fair that crying turned her dark pink, which made Nadine giggle. How cute she looked, thought Nadine, so different from herself. The older girl would lay her dark fingers between the baby's light ones and sing 'night and day, night and day, night and day'. She especially liked it when their mother eased the baby on to her lap and handed her its warm bottle. The sisters bonded.

The next year, Nadine began school. She hated having to leave her sister at home but soon grew accustomed to other children, and even liked them. She learned quickly and teachers told Mrs Lutter she had raised 'a treasure'. The girl was as loving to her classmates as if they were her own sisters and brothers. If other children lost pencils or gloves, Nadine led the search and usually found the missing item. If someone couldn't tie their shoes, Nadine immediately knelt down and pressed her little finger on the knot to hold it steady. But the kid she most enjoyed taking care of was not in her class but at home, and every afternoon she raced back to be with her. With a hard-working husband who had little time for child-rearing, Mrs Lutter was grateful to have Nadine play second parent to the younger girl.

In turn, Dale grew up adoring her big sister. She loved horsey rides on Nadine's back. She loved building tents from sheets and camping with her in the living room. But most of all, she loved it when Nadine read stories to her at bedtime. As they lay facing one another in the bed they insisted on sharing, Dale played with her sister's thick, soft hair that she so envied. Nadine assured her that short curls were just as pretty. When they pressed their mother on the question, Mrs Lutter wrote them a poem.

Nadine's skin is night and her hair, a dark river.
Dale's skin is light and her hair, a cluster of grapes.
My beautiful two.
Different as the parents they came through.

Then came Dale's turn to go out into the world and she brought it back to her mirror. One evening at the dinner table the little girl announced that she was the pretty sister. Nadine stopped chewing. Mrs Lutter smiled and patted her daughter's hand. Don't be silly, she said. Oh, but I am the pretty one, Mommy, the child insisted, her innocent eyes big with excitement. Her teacher had said so. Nadine would be pretty too if she had light skin.

Mrs Lutter's mouth dropped open at the same moment Mr Lutter's fist dropped on to the table. Nadine stared at the dusky skin and straight hair of her mother. Then at the fair skin and nappy hair of her father. And then at the beige skin and bushy hair of her sister. Before her father could grab her hand, she ran from the table and it took her mother a lot of coaxing to get her back. And a great deal of consoling by their father to stop Dale from blubbering tearfully about not meaning to be a bad girl. The subject was changed and not ever, warned Mr Lutter, to be brought up again. The Lutter family finished dinner, ate dessert and did dishes together before going to bed.

That night, the parents agreed to write a letter of complaint to the school principal. It was outrageous, they whispered, a teacher saying such a thing to a child. And a black teacher at that. What was her problem?

You wouldn't think she had one, said Mrs Lutter who'd met her once, with all her black pride talk. Well, the school would definitely hear about this.

In the children's room Dale slept snuggled at Nadine's back, her fingers tangled in her sister's hair. Nadine lay wide awake, staring at the darkness. Why did Miss Whitman say that? She touched her face, traced around the flare of her nose, the curve of her lips. She was pretty. Wasn't she? Mom and Dad had always said so. The pale moon sat high in the black sky. In its light, she examined her thin arm, brown as the chocolate ice cream she so loved. Never before had she looked at her skin in that way, scrutinizing it as if for some awful secret it held. It was dark, even darker than Mom's. Maybe they'd only said she was pretty, to protect her. Nadine sighed and shut her eyes against the night.

As the girls grew, so did their worries, fears and finally obsessions about their looks. Mornings they stood side by side at the wide bathroom mirror. Dale splashed her light face with water and Nadine scrubbed her dark one with soap. Nadine swept her hair with a soft-bristled brush and Dale yanked through hers with an afro pick. Like spies, they observed each other's reflections in secret, pretending to look straight ahead at their own. Nadine was proud of her mane, hair her girlfriends complimented for its glamorous length and silky feel. Dale grew grateful for her 'gorgeous light' skin, words she came to believe meant the same thing. Their relationship suffered as the wound inflicted by the world outside bled the happiness from the girls they'd been on the inside. Tension usurped tenderness. Competition squashed camaraderie. And finally, inevitably, antagonism replaced affection.

And then came, as naturally as night follows day, rage. It was Nadine's first day in the sixth grade and she'd been assigned to Mr Hill's homeroom class. She was as overjoyed as any young girl in love with her teacher would be, having developed a crush the instant he passed her in the hallway and left a trail of heat in her face. A homeroom adviser to the older kids and arithmetic teacher of the younger ones, her sister had been in his class the year before.

Nadine rushed to the front of the first row, the desk nearest Mr Hill's, and sat down. He began by checking attendance, calling names in alphabetical order. One after another, girls and boys raised hands. Here! Present! Yeah! Nadine's stomach was in knots as he made his way through the Ls. Larson? Levine? Lincoln?

The moment when their eyes would meet and their mouths smile suddenly arrived. Lutter?

She answered that she was 'here', horrified that her voice had come out kind of croaky. He smiled and asked if she was related to Dale Lutter, the pretty little second-grader? Irritated at the mention of her sister, she smiled and said yeah. At least, his eyes were on *her*.

Amazing, was what he said, you two don't look at all alike. Then he just kept on reading the names like nothing bad had happened. Lyons? Matthews? McDonnell?

She was sullen for the rest of class, scribbling in her notebook: I hate Mr Hill, I hate Mr Hill, I hate Mr Hill.

Instead of attending homeroom, she hung out in

the schoolyard with friends, telling 'ya mama so black' jokes. Ya mama so black, they howled, she got lost in the tunnel of love. Ya daddy couldn't see her on their black satin sheets. She was the shadow in the movie *Dark Shadow*. The cops couldn't even see her with night-vision goggles. Nadine laughed and laughed and laughed, loud and hard, that is until 'ya mama' became 'you', then she pounded her fists into the kids' faces and scratched and bit at their skin. Detention after school and punishment at home became commonplace. And while grounded she occupied herself devising names for her sister – High Yella, Piss-coloured, Zebra Girl – whose skin colour pricked her hurt feelings like a cactus. But once she saw Dale's reaction to the name Zebra Girl, she knew she had hit on something good.

Dale had always loved summertime. Every day she stayed outside until the sky turned deep red. With a headband around her thick hair and wearing her favourite blue shorts and white socks, she delighted in double dutch, boxball and all the fun things city sidewalks provided.

One day towards the end of summer she was in her room reading. The girls had long been separated because of their constant fighting and now had their own rooms. It was too hot even for an undershirt or socks and Dale wore none. Nadine pushed open the door without knocking and stretched out on the floor.

Dale knew her big sister didn't like her any more from the way she always teased and made fun of her. But she didn't know what she had done. Mrs Lutter had advised her to be extra nice because Nadine was having a hard time being a teenager. She had tried, but it seemed to make Nadine meaner. So she gave up and told herself the nice sister, the one she had so loved and who loved her, had been kidnapped by monsters who'd left a mean, fake one in her place.

Dale asked her what she wanted. As usual, she wanted to show off. She told her sister to check out her nails and stuck her hand right in front of the page Dale was reading. The nails were long and covered with polka dots. Yeah, answered Dale, still reading. That was when Nadine pointed at her feet and shrieked. Beige legs and white feet! Like zebra stripes, the older girl howled. What a freak! Dale stared at her pale feet and her brown legs and burst into tears. For a second Nadine felt bad, but it quickly passed and soon she had some of the kids at school calling her sister Zebra Girl.

Mrs Lutter removed her woollen hat and gloves, now caked with ice, and slapped them against each other. She blinked snow from her lashes.

'Dale, are you crazy? What were you doing hanging your bare feet out the window in this freezing weather? Come over here, look how you're shaking.'

She pulled her daughter closer and knelt before her. The bottom of the girl's pyjamas were cuffed just above her bony ankles. Her feet felt like narrow blocks of ice and her legs, hands and face were ice cold.

'For crying out loud,' exclaimed Mrs Lutter, staring at the blue toes, 'how long were you sitting there in that cold? Don't you know that's how you catch pneumonia?'

She sat Dale down on a kitchen chair and began furiously rubbing her daughter's feet. 'Are your lips frozen together too? Answer me!'

Dale's feet were stinging. She didn't know if it was from the cold or from the rubbing, which was beginning to hurt.

'I don't know how long. From when you went out I guess.'

'That was nearly two hours ago, Dale!' She rubbed faster, feeling panicky. The girl had no meat on her bones as it was and was forever coming down with something. Sitting in a cold window like a lunatic . . . why, half the neighbourhood was sneezing and coughing, and those were folks who at least had enough sense to try to stay warm! 'Why on earth . . . what were you doing?'

'Owww,' moaned Dale, 'you're hurting them.'

Mrs Lutter got an old baby blanket from the closet and wrapped it around Dale's feet. She sat on a chair. 'Don't make me lose my patience, Dale Frances!'

More than not wanting to say why because it was stupid, Dale didn't want her mother hollering at her.

'Tanning.'

Mrs Lutter looked at Dale, shook her head as if the movement would help her understand what the girl had just said, and looked down at the ball of blanket.

'Tanning? Your feet? In the cold?'

'Look at them,' Dale said, kicking off the blanket and swallowing hard, 'they're lighter than my legs.'

'Of course they are. When it's hot out you wear shorts and sneakers. The sun only hits your legs. For the life of me, if that's not the silliest thing . . .'

She began to rub Dale's feet again. Dale snatched them away.

'Can't you see, Mom, they're white and ugly and don't match! Like a zebra.'

She shut her eyes tight but her tears fell anyway. She sobbed so that it startled her mother, who pulled her closer.

'Don't cry like that, honey, look at you, you're getting yourself all worked up. Your feet are not ugly! Your father's feet are light too. Are Daddy's feet ugly?'

Dale could barely catch her breath. She was almost choking on the pain she'd swallowed year after year.

'Dale Frances Lutter, now you listen to your mother! You are a beautiful little girl from your head right down to your toes. Where'd you get all this nonsense? You know I told you about paying attention to the foolishness the kids in school come up with. Your family is who you should be listening to, we're the ones who love you and will tell you the truth. How many times has Mommy said that, sweetheart?'

'A hundred times,' sobbed Dale, 'and Nadine calls me Zebra Girl a hundred times a day!'

'What? Zebra Girl? If I've told that girl once I've told her a hundred times, I will not have you girls calling each other names!'

Mrs Lutter wrapped her arms around Dale's trembling shoulders. As soon as she could speak again Dale begged her mother not to get her in trouble with Nadine by saying anything.

'If she knew how bad she makes you feel she'd feel

awful. You know, when people feel bad themselves sometimes it overflows and spills on whoever's closest. Your sister loves you.'

'No she doesn't,' responded Dale, her head still resting on her mother's shoulder, 'she hates me because I'm high yella and the colour of piss and have feet that aren't the same colour as my legs.' An icy cold had settled inside her bones. She shivered.

Mrs Lutter patted Dale's puffy hair but said nothing. Her pretty girls, fighting over skin colour . . . she could hardly believe it. Hadn't they loved them both the same, taught them to see beauty in difference? Lots of black families ran the colour gamut, from off-white to butter pecan to ink black. Some people said it came from white slave-owners who abused women slaves and passed their blood down through the generations. She had friends with a house full of kids, and not two of them the same colour. It was just part of being black. You tried to raise your children around it, teach them not to be colour-struck. If there'd been a colour problem with some white kid at the school, that she'd expect and know how to deal with. But between her babies? The Lutters were going to have to tackle this one as a family. But first she had to get her little girl under a pile of blankets. The child was already sniffling and snivelling something terrible.

'Where's Dale?' asked Nadine.

The sky was purple with evening light and they always had to be home by dusk. The empty chair at the dinner table meant nobody to sneak frowns at or kick her foot against. Her parents glanced at each other, looked at their daughter and cleared their throats. Then neither said a word. Dale was where she'd been since that morning, tucked in her bed with a hot-water bottle, coughing, sneezing and sweating. A neighbour who worked in a clinic had dropped by during her lunch hour to take a look at the girl. Watch her, she'd said, and left syrups, salves and children's aspirin. Mr Lutter's foot tapped his wife's. They'd agreed she should be the one to begin because he might lose his temper. She tore off a piece of garlic bread.

'Your sister's not feeling well and is in bed. She spent a good part of the morning alone in her room with her windows wide open. Whatever happened to you two playing together?'

Mr Lutter turned a swirl of spaghetti round on his fork without lifting it to his mouth.

'Right, it's like freezing out and she has her windows open. Duh! And Mom, I'm sixteen, OK? *Play?* I don't think so.'

'I think your mother's saying you should spend more time with your sister like you used to. Be a big sister, for a change.'

'Remember when you two were best friends,' interjected Mrs Lutter, feeling her husband's temper heating up, 'you'd spend hours talking and giggling in your little tent. Remember, Nadine? You two were adorable.'

Mr Lutter said, 'You know, Nadine, you girls only have each other. Your mother and I won't be here forever.' The mound of spaghetti twirled in a circle.

Nadine pursed her mouth, sucked up a long string of

13

spaghetti and licked from her lips a small bouquet of tomato sauce.

'Whatever.'

Mr Lutter's fork clinked hard on his plate. He hated it when she said that. Mrs Lutter pressed her foot hard on his.

'She's sick, honey,' said Mrs Lutter, still holding the torn-off piece of garlic bread. 'I even asked Miss Paulie – you know her, the nurse's aide – to come by. She has a bad head cold.'

Nadine was beginning to feel sick too – of all the drama around Dale's little cold.

'Well, that's really sad and everything but hellooo, who sits in front of an open window when there's a snow blizzard just watching the birds fly by?' She dangled a spaghetti string from her lips, then sucked it in.

'Zebra Girl, that's who,' answered her mother, tossing the bread on the table. Mr Lutter left his fork upright in his spaghetti.

Nadine felt her face flush with heat. She flashed back on Dale bursting out crying the first time she called her that. She coughed. A small clump of food hit her chest. She wiped it off and at the same time wiped that memory from her thoughts. So that's why they were acting so weird, she realized, pale Dale had gone whining to them just to get her grounded. And she was supposed to go to the movies with Ray! Damn.

'If there's anything your mother and I have tried to teach you girls it's that tearing each other down with insults and nasty names is a trap. There's a world of

14

people outside these doors all too eager to do that to each and every one of us. We should not be helping them. I listen to that crap all day long at the plant and I'm not going to listen to it in this family, do you hear me, Nadine?'

'Sir, yes, sir!' shouted the teenager, saluting.

That did it. His fist slammed on the table and Nadine jumped in her chair.

'This is not a joke, miss!'

'Why's everything my fault?' she yelled, springing to her feet, 'I didn't tell her to sunbathe in a snowstorm! How's that my fault?' She may have taken her looks from her mother, but Nadine's temper was as hot as her father's.

'Sit down!' ordered Mr Lutter.

Mrs Lutter placed her hand on Nadine's. 'Dale was holding her feet out the window to tan them because you told her she looked like a zebra with different-coloured feet and legs. She's your little sister, Nadine, and she's hurting. From names you call her – High Yella and Piss-coloured and the rest of the mess . . .'

Nadine snatched her hand away. Her eyes were wet. 'And what about me? You think I'm not hurt too, my whole life hearing how pretty Dale's skin is, how light, how fair, how whatever! Why's it OK for everyone to tease me about being burnt and charcoal . . . and . . . black! If I didn't have this hair to make up for being so dark I wouldn't even have Ray! He said that!'

Mr Lutter grabbed his daughter's wrist. 'Then your little boyfriend Ray is an idiot! You're a beautiful girl, all of you is beautiful. Those idiots teasing you are

15

screwed-up kids who probably can't stand the sight of their own faces in the mirror. Direct your anger at them, not at Dale. She needs you.'

'But, Daddy,' cried the teenager, burying her head in his shoulder, 'I can't help feeling like it's her fault. If she weren't around, people couldn't compare us, it's horrible what they say. And I'm always the loser.'

Nadine cried like the little child she really was. The Lutters sat talking until the sky had grown black as onyx. For much of it, Nadine sat quietly between her parents, looking down and nodding. When she talked, her voice was soft and sad, full of stories of hurt. First one parent, then the other, would place a comforting hand beneath her chin and raise her head. Look at me, they said, you're perfect as you are.

Soon it was time for them all to turn in. They all kissed and hugged and the parents retired to their bedroom. Nadine headed to hers. She stopped outside Dale's door, thought a moment, then went on to her own room. She turned on the TV to the music channel, then turned it off. She looked at the windowpane where her finger had traced the names 'Nay' and 'Ray'. The letters were runny and smeared like a tear-streaked face. With her palm she wiped the window clean. She sat on her stool and looked at the walls of her room, papered with images of girls who sang and danced and acted, every one the colour of honey. Nowhere did she see a face like her own. She reached for a small, framed photograph propped on the corner of her desk. Two little girls grinned, their arms draped around each other's shoulders, one the colour of golden syrup, the other the colour of rich molasses, both as cute as they could be. She smiled at herself and her sister. She kissed them both. Then she wept.

The next morning, she crept into Dale's room. Having slept through an entire day, the little girl was awake despite the early hour. She heard a noise and rose up on her elbow. Trouble, she thought. Mom had probably got on Nadine about Zebra Girl, and now Nadine was going to get her back.

'What?' she said anxiously.

'You awake?'

'Yeah. But I'm sick so don't bother me. What?'

Nadine sat on the edge of the bed. 'How're your feet doing?'

Dale didn't answer. Nadine reached under the blanket.

'Hmmm, you still got 'em.'

'Leave me alone. I didn't mean to tell. It just popped out.'

'Listen. I'm really sorry about all that. I mean calling them names and calling you names and everything. I took stuff out on you that I shouldn't have just because kids were being mean to me.'

Dale kept quiet. Was Nadine going to smack her on the head and say 'sucker!'? But Nadine didn't say anything at all, she just sat there looking at the blanket.

'Really?'

'Really. You're a great sister. And your feet are great too.'

'They are?'

'Yeah.'

17

Dale got an idea. 'Then kiss them.'

'No! Ugh! They're not that great!'

The sisters' laughter woke their parents, who looked at each other quizzically.

Nadine had been so mean for so long that Dale's feelings flew in one direction then the other. Had the monsters finally brought her real sister back or was the fake one trying to trick her? Nadine looked in her little sister's face and saw the baby with the big eyes and fat cheeks, now looking back at her with a mixture of hope and fear. How could she have treated her so badly? As if reading her mind, Dale had a question.

'Nadine . . . why are you so mean all the time? What did I do to make you stop liking me?'

'I'm sorry, Dale.'

'I know. But I just wanna know what I did so I won't do it again and make you mad at me again.'

The black jokes and Mr Hill and Ray rushed towards her like ghosts in a Haunted House amusement park ride. She knew the little girl lying in bed had nothing to do with it but still, she couldn't look at her without feeling the things those other people made her feel. She didn't understand it herself so how could she explain it to a twelve-year-old? She couldn't.

'You didn't do anything. And don't worry, you can't do anything to make me stop liking you. Sometimes things get confusing and you don't feel good any more and you don't want to talk about it because saying it out loud makes you feel worse so you just act up.'

'You can talk to me. I get confused too.'

Nadine smiled and put her hand on her sister's head

like she used to when they'd be in their home-made tent.

'OK, Dale, I'll talk to you.'

'OK.'

She kissed Dale's cheek. 'And you talk to me too if I'm being a jerk or something.'

The Lutter girls hung out in Dale's room for the rest of the day, doing puzzles, telling stories and watching television. It was as though they were afraid to leave and risk breaking the spell of the moment. The world outside that room had not changed. Maybe the world inside them would.

Janet McDonald grew up in Brooklyn, New York. She is a lawyer and the author of the memoir Project Girl *and the urban trilogy* Spellbound, Chill Wind *and* Twists and Turns, *and lives in Paris, France.*

The Blokes

by Alan Gibbons

To Robert Cormier, an inspirational writer

*A story set in the present day in the north
of England*

There are these people. They've got something on me.
In turn, I've got something on one of the refugee boys,
Hashim. Now, being new, Hashim doesn't have anything on anybody. He's just trying to learn the ropes. He
wants to fit in, but it isn't that easy, not at my school.
That's the way it is with newcomers, they're outside the
loop, vulnerable. It's also what makes Hashim the weakest link, the one that can be broken, the one I've been
ordered to break.

I seem to have started in the middle of my story
so maybe it's best to jump back to the beginning. I'm
John Keenan. I guess I'd better explain about the
people who are blackmailing me. They're called The
Blokes. The Blokes are maybe half a dozen kids, ten at
most, who pull the strings at my school. You wouldn't
think so few could be so powerful, but The Blokes are.
They say what goes, who is to be pulled into the inner

20

circle, who is to be kept out, who is to be broken. And they've decided Hashim has to be broken.

So be it.

The main thing about The Blokes is that they are English. Add that to the fact that they are white and, well, *blokes*, and you pretty much have it. Girls are decoration only, totty. As for the black kids and the asylum seekers, they'll never be part of the inner circle. The inner circle is strictly whites only. English, you see, equals white. There ain't no black in the Union Jack, that's how The Blokes think. Top and bottom of it is, The Blokes are as British as fish and chips, bulldog tattoos and a thump in the kidneys.

Though I only became aware of their presence at the start of the autumn term, it seems The Blokes were founded when the first asylum seekers arrived, when *they* entered *our* school. That's when the graffiti started, little St George flags over-written with their name, The Blokes. Most people thought it was a pop group at first, then we started hearing about the sanctions.

There's this Chinese kid in Year Seven, Peter Fong. As far as I can make out, he was the first victim. He's brainy, quiet and good at music, which is three strokes against him as far as The Blokes are concerned. Peter got the Head Teacher's Award for his music at the end of November. His whole family came to the assembly to see him receive it. They were so proud of Peter, it just came oozing out of them. That's probably what did it, this show of pride, because at the start of December, Peter got an early Christmas present. The Blokes frightened one of Peter's friends into handing over his clarinet. That's how they work, playing kids off against each other, divide and rule. When they got their hands on the instrument they stamped on it and bent it completely out of shape.

The Fongs came in to complain but Peter got worked over a couple of times and had his head flushed down the boys' toilet so the complaints stopped. That pride of theirs, it turned out to be like an apple with a maggot inside. Peter was victim number one, but he definitely isn't going to be the last.

Since that first sanction, The Blokes have been getting more and more active. One Sikh family even took their kids out of school two weeks ago and moved them elsewhere. We all watched them go on the last day, feeling sorry for them, but we couldn't help feeling glad we weren't in their shoes.

I know what you're thinking, what do I need to worry about? I'm white so why would The Blokes pick on me? But that's the whole point. The way they see it, there are three camps in school. There are The Blokes. There are The Blokes' targets, the black kids and the asylum seekers. Then there's the rest, the white kids that just want to keep their heads down and survive. Which is exactly why The Blokes have got me in their sights: I'm one of the quiet kids who try to go with the flow. I don't have anything against anybody. The trouble is, in The Blokes' eyes, there's no sitting on the fence. As Andy Ball, The Blokes' big cheese, once said to me: 'You're either with us or you're against us.' And, because I dared to make friends with Hashim, I was against them until I proved otherwise.

So what's the big deal, you're probably wondering. Hashim's your friend. Tell The Blokes to take a running jump at themselves. OK, so they might give you a bit of aggravation. Big deal, it's not the end of the world. But it isn't that easy. Life never is. It's like I tried to explain earlier, The Blokes have got something on me.

Something big.

It's my dad. He killed a kid.

He didn't mean to. He was doing thirty in a thirty mile an hour zone. He wasn't speeding. The kid just stepped out. Nothing Dad could do. It doesn't matter that he's innocent though, does it? The kid's family couldn't accept that it wasn't my dad's fault. They started following him, making threats. I can understand it, I suppose. They'd lost their little boy. But it made life hard for us. Mum wanted to stay and stick it out. Dad wouldn't listen though. He'd had enough. He wanted to get away. That's why we moved houses and I ended up in my new school.

So there you go. That's what The Blokes have got on me.

Here's what Andy Ball said to me the day after my mate Paul spilled his guts:

'A little birdy tells me your dad's a murderer.'

Yes, just like that. I looked round at the other kids in the corridor, but they didn't hear. They were keeping well clear. Well, you would if you saw Andy Ball and two of his lieutenants corner somebody. I made sure nobody was listening then stared at Andy, willing him to keep his voice down.

'What?'

'You heard,' Andy said. 'A kid-killer, how low can you get?'

'He didn't do anything wrong,' I cried. 'It was an accident.'

My skin was burning all the way down my spine. The Blokes had their claws in me. I belonged to them now. Can you imagine what that's like? I seemed to have toppled right off the edge of the world.

Andy smirked.

'Sure,' he chuckled. 'That's what they all say.'

His acid words were burning down to the bone. I was dying of shame, Dad's shame.

'It's true,' I told him.

'True or false,' Andy said, 'I bet you don't want it getting round. A kid-killer for a dad. Can't be good for the image, can it? We can keep quiet about it, of course, for a price.'

'What do you want?' I asked.

'Nothing just now,' Andy said. 'But I'll be calling in the favour.'

He took a few steps then glanced back.

'Soon.'

So that's how things stood. Until two weeks ago. That's when Mrs Jones came up with her big idea. She wanted to make the new kids, the refugees from Kosovo, welcome. She came up with the idea of a competition, *Where I'm From*. The plan is you make something: a poster, a map, a model, a sculpture – something that celebrates your roots. Jenny Bruce was born in Scotland

24

so she is making the St Andrew's flag out of mosaic. Paul Lenahan is a Scouser so he's making a Liver Bird out of papier mâché. I won't bore you with the rest. You've got the picture by now. The point is, everybody knows who is going to win.

Hashim.

He's brilliant with his hands. You've never seen anything like it. He's like that Midas fellow, everything he touches turns to gold. Most of the kids think Mrs Jones made up the competition just for Hashim; a way of making him feel at home here. They've got a point. The Kosovans have had a hard time. The council stuck them in a run-down tower block over on the north side of town and they've had nothing but aggravation. Mrs Jones wants to do something to make amends, but she isn't doing Hashim any favours. The Blokes have got wind of the whole thing and they plan to come down hard on him.

Which is where I come in.

Hashim trusts me, you see. We've become big mates. Hashim even suggested keeping his model at my house – closer to the school so it's less likely to get damaged on the way. I think what he really means is not damaged by some of the characters on his estate. Plus, his flat is so poky you can't swing a cat, never mind build a village. That's what he's doing, by the way, building a scale model of his village, the one he left back in Kosovo. Soldiers came and burned all the houses and ripped down the mosque. That's all Hashim will say but I know he saw stuff, bad stuff. The kind of stuff The Blokes can only dream of doing one day.

I'm just scared The Blokes will find out where Hashim keeps his village. Because I know what they'll do to it. They'll remind me that whoever isn't with them is against them.

And they'll make me betray my friend.

I'm waiting for Hashim at home time when I hear Andy Ball's voice.

'Hey, Piggy,' he says. 'How's the model going?'

They call Hashim Piggy, you see, as in 'The Three Pigs', houses of sticks and straw and all that. They think they're really witty.

Ignore them, I think, willing Hashim to keep walking. *Don't talk to them.*

'It's good,' says Hashim, smiling uncertainly. He knows all about Andy Ball. Maybe he's thinking Andy's turned over a new leaf. Fat chance. If you're a Bloke, the leaf only lies one way.

'Yes?' says Andy, glancing in my direction. 'Tell me about it.'

'I used Mod-roc,' Hashim explains. 'From the Mod-roc I made mountains.'

'Mountains, eh?' says Andy, his eyes twinkling.

'Yes, I cover them with a green material called flock so that they look real. And on the mountains I have built tiny houses. They look like . . .'

Hashim looks at me for the word.

'Chalets,' I say. 'Toblerone houses.'

'Yes,' says Hashim, loving the sound of the word. 'Toblerone.'

'So you're going to paint them?' asks Andy.

'Yes, the houses will be white and the roofs will be red. They will stand out against the green of the mountains. Finally, I will have a mosque at the end of the main street.'

'Right,' says Andy, nudging one of his mates in the ribs. 'A mosque.'

Hashim frowns. His smile has evaporated.

'I'm going now,' he says. 'With John.'

'Yes, that's right,' says Andy. 'You run along with your good friend John.'

Hashim frowns. Me too.

An hour later I'm helping Hashim paint his houses. He has brought these really fine brushes from home. My hand won't keep still and I almost mess it up.

'No,' says Hashim, patient but firm. 'You must go slowly, like this.'

Hashim smiles. He has made some good stuff before, but this is his masterpiece. He made the other models with his hands and his brain. This village comes straight from his heart.

Now The Blokes want me to break it.

The next day The Blokes make their move. They corner me in the dining hall.

'I hear you're helping Piggy with his model,' says Andy.

'His name is Hashim,' I say.

'I know what he's called,' says Andy. 'And you know what you're going to do.'

'Do I?'

Andy brings his face close to mine.

'You really want me to spell it out?' he asks.

When I don't answer he produces a matchbox from his pocket.

'Let's say this is one of Hashim's little houses, his chalets. Well,' he continues, 'we were wondering what was wrong with English houses.'

'Hashim doesn't come from England,' I say, as if things are that simple.

'So this is what you're going to do for us,' Andy says, resting the matchbox on his palm. 'You're going to take every one of Piggy's chalets, his cute little Toblerone houses . . . and you're going to squash them flat.'

Andy puts the matchbox down on the table and crushes it with his palm.

'After all, we don't want Daddy getting a bad name, do we?'

I don't sleep too well that night.

After an hour of tossing and turning I get up and go downstairs. I go in the back room and look at Hashim's village. We finished the houses this evening. Just the mosque to go. The curtains are open and there is a full moon. The unworldly light falls on the white of the house walls and they seem to glow against the deep, almost blackish, green of the mountains. I try to imagine what it was like when the soldiers came. Hashim once told me it was after dark, on a moonlit night just like this. I look at the village and imagine the running feet, the bursts of gunfire, the fires. I imagine the soldiers blowing all the Toblerone houses down, just like the Big Bad Wolf.

I'm still thinking that way when Dad appears.

'What's up, son? Can't sleep?'

I shake my head.

'Anything on your mind?' he asks. 'I've had my fair share of sleepless nights.'

He means the accident, of course.

'No,' I say. 'Nothing wrong.'

I could get good at lying.

The next day Andy is waiting at the school gates. When he finds out that I haven't done it yet, he reminds me what The Blokes want.

'Competition day tomorrow,' he says. 'Tonight's the night.'

'I know,' I say.

'Just checking,' says Andy.

He gives me a long, hard look, as if he's mulling something over, then walks off with his friends. Soon I'm joined by Hashim.

'Can I come round to finish the mosque?' he asks. 'It's my last chance to get it just right. Competition day tomorrow.'

'Yes,' I say. 'I know.'

We are putting the finishing touches to the mosque at about half past seven.

'Was the mosque's roof really gold?' I ask, watching Hashim carefully applying the second coat of gold paint.

'No,' says Hashim. 'But it should have been.'

I can't think of anything to say so I change the subject.

'We'll be finished in a few minutes,' I say.

The evening light is falling on the village, just like the moonlight did last night. In the dark it was the soldiers I could see. Now, by the light of the setting sun, I can see mothers putting their kids to bed, farmers on their way home from the fields.

I'm sorry, Hashim. So sorry.

Hashim looks at me.

'You're quiet,' he says.

'Yes,' I say.

My throat is so tight I can hardly speak. Just then Dad pops his head round the door and offers Hashim a lift home.

Ten minutes later I've got tears in my eyes and there's a big, black hole inside me. The houses are crushed, the shell of the mosque split in two. I've done it. I've done The Blokes' dirty work. Then Dad comes in to see if I want some supper.

'John!' he cries. 'What have you done?'

So I explain. It comes tumbling out, every bit of my shame and humiliation.

'Oh, John,' says Dad, shaking his head.

'You mean, you think I did the wrong thing?'

'I know you did.'

'But they would have told,' I cry. 'Everybody would know what you did.'

'So what?' says Dad.

I can't believe what I'm hearing.

'Look, son,' Dad says. 'I was wrong. I should have stayed and stood up for myself, the way your mother wanted me to. It's time you did the same. You've got to phone Hashim and own up to what you've done.'

When I phone Hashim his voice dies at the end of the line. He hangs up without a word. Then, ten minutes later, he's back on the phone.

'I will come round at half past seven in the morning,' he says. 'I have things to do.'

'But it's ruined,' I say. 'Broken to bits. I'm really sorry . . .'

'Do the mountains still stand?' he asks.

'Yes, but . . .'

'Then I will be round early.'

Hashim doesn't want me in the room.

'What's he doing?' Mum asks.

I shrug. Hashim isn't talking. His face is like a mask. His eyes are like black stones. But he isn't beaten. That's what I don't understand. The Blokes haven't broken him the way they broke me.

'Hashim,' I say, knocking on the door. 'Can I help in any way?'

'No,' he says. 'Just give me some more time.'

It is twenty to nine when he finally opens the door. I can't see what he's done. The model is Sellotaped in two black bin bags.

'Are we late?' he asks.

'Don't worry about that,' Mum says. 'I'll give you a lift in for once.'

31

I can tell that she's impressed. Whatever Hashim has done, he has chosen to face up to The Blokes.

It is half past eleven and people are unwrapping their models in the hall. The Blokes are watching. Andy tries to catch my eye but I stare straight through him.

I go over to Hashim, hoping he doesn't tell me to leave him alone.

'But what have you done?' I ask. 'There wasn't time to rebuild it.'

'I didn't try,' says Hashim.

Then, without another word, he removes the bin bags from around his model.

Mrs Jones hesitates for a moment then says, 'Oh, Hashim.'

The shell of the mosque is still broken. The houses are still crushed. But Hashim has rubbed charcoal into the white walls so that they look charred, as if by fire. He has removed what was left of the red-tiled roofs and left the Toblerone homes open to the sky. Finally, here and there, he has pasted on red and orange tissue paper so that it looks like flames licking the shattered buildings. Tiny horses, painstakingly carved from wood, lie dead on the road.

'This is my village,' Hashim says, meeting the eyes first of Mrs Jones then of Andy.

'This is the truth.'

Five days later The Blokes haven't said a word about Dad. Maybe they will and maybe they won't. I'm not sure it matters. They know I'm ready to tough it out.

So is Dad. You can only scare someone who is ready to be afraid. As for Hashim, I'm going bowling with him tonight. That was his prize for winning the competition with his village.

When he asked me to go with him I could hardly believe it.

'You mean we're still friends?' I said. 'After what I did.'

You know what Hashim said then?

'It was your hands broke the village,' he told me. 'But they were moved by the badness in the hearts of others.'

It seems The Blokes got Hashim wrong.

He isn't the weakest link.

He's the strongest.

Alan Gibbons was born in Cheshire. He has written over thirty books for children and teenagers. He now lives in Liverpool with his wife and four children. He has won a Blue Peter Book Award and twice been shortlisted for the Carnegie Medal.

The Pavee and the Buffer

by Siobhan Dowd

A story set in present-day Ireland

'Don't go digging up troubles,' his mam called as he set off. 'You and your da, you're the one pair. Digging up troubles like bad old potatoes.'

Jim turned back and waved, catching her in a smile. Her old yellow frock flapped in the June wind, matching the Calor gas bottles around the trailers.

'Aways with you,' she said.

He went down the steep hill towards Dundray. As the morning haze thinned, he could make out the speckled dots of houses and a faint trace of the pier from the white shimmer of sea. Somewhere down there was the school. He'd have given anything not to go. But the education people had been around three times waving papers and mouthing the law, and his mam and da had given in.

'It'll only be a few weeks, Jimmy,' his da said. 'Then you can come scrapping again.'

'The Buffers may be better down there,' his mam

said. 'Try and get a few words of the reading off them.'

In the last school, a year ago, he'd picked up a black eye and a bruised collarbone in two weeks, but no reading. The thought of all those books with the ugly black marks like secret codes was worse than all the fights put together. He paused, wondering if he should jump over the hedge and run for it, but his Uncle Mirt pulled up behind him in the van. 'Are yous off down that Buffer school too?' he said.

'S'pose.'

'Hop in. I'll drop you at the gate with the others.'

He climbed in the back where his cousins crouched, their faces dropping to the South Pole.

'I've never bin to secondary school before,' said young Declan. He wheezed with the asthma and took out his spray.

'It's the pits,' said May. Lil mimed a doom-laden spit.

'It's worse than the pits,' said Jim. 'Give me a mine to go down any day.'

'What's it like so, Jimmy, if it's worse than the pits?' said Declan.

'It's like a laboratory run by robots. And we're the rats. The ones they give electric shocks to as an experiment.' The van lurched over a hump in the road and came to a stop. 'And it smells like a bit of cheese from the last century – any decent rat would turn up its nose.'

'We're here,' said Uncle Mirt. 'Out yous all get and no malarkying.'

But he beckoned Jim over and whispered, 'Would you ever keep an eye out for young Declan? The

35

wheezing's been wicked bad of late.' Jim nodded and followed the others through the school gates.

They stood in a line staring across the grounds at the huddles of maroon uniforms. Jim glanced towards Declan. He could hardly see his face for the freckles, but he could tell that he was frightened from the way he stood so close. A gang lounging near the hurling hut drifted over. When they were within range, one of them said, 'They look like brown smut. My dad says that's what they are.'

'Whisht, they might put a curse on us,' another hissed.

Jim felt like baring his teeth and crossing his two forefingers into a blasphemous crucifix, to give them something to think about. But his mam's 'don't-go-digging-troubles' voice rang in his head. He looked away, and found himself locked in a gaze with a different girl, who stood on her own. She was chubby, with bright high bunches. Her uniform was baggy, her socks down around her ankles. She half smiled, half shrugged at him, and then stared upwards as if the whole school was a show. He thought about stepping over to say hello, but as he put his foot forward, it was as if a force-field stopped him, his da telling him to keep away. 'Don't go messing with any Buffers. They're all the same. They hate us Pavees. Do your business with them and walk away.'

A bell rang. The school filed into the gym for assembly like maroon ants. Jim tried a devil-may-care saunter, miming a whistle, but all around the stares were coming at him, so he fixed his eyes to the linoleum and tried to vanish instead. He felt a right bad thumb in his old dark suit, however long his mam had pressed it. Someone handed him a hymnbook and when everyone started singing about Love Divine coming down, he pretended to join in. He knew he had the book the right way up; he'd learned that much. But he didn't know the right page, so he kept the book in a narrow crack, close to his nose. Then they filed out to various classrooms. In his, the form teacher was waiting, sitting back on his dais, tapping his pen on the register.

'You,' he said. 'Sit here.' He indicated a vacant seat in the front row. It was next to the lone girl from the playground.

There was silence as the teacher looked around, marking off names in the register.

'Where's Leahy?' he said.

'He's still got the flu, Mr Tassey,' said someone.

'It's a strange flu altogether,' he said, 'this summer flu. You, the new boy. Stand up and tell us who you are.'

'Me?' said Jim.

'Who else?'

Jim stood up and looked around the class. There were smirks and boredom, curiosity, expectant shuffles.

'I'm me,' he said at last. There were sniggers.

'Your name,' said Mr Tassey. 'You must know that much.'

'Which one?' said Jim.

'All of them!'

'Only, sees, I was baptized six times. James Jonathan

37

Jeremiah. Joseph Jacob Jonas. Curran. They call me Big J in camp. But Jim Curran's fine.'

'Well, Jim Curran,' said Mr Tassey. 'Sit down and less blackguarding. Understood?'

He sat down, but when the teacher had turned his back he rolled his eyes around in their sockets. The girl next to him grinned. He caught her eye and winked. She scribbled something on her exercise book and showed it to him. It was a cartoon of the teacher. His big chin and nose poked out like Popeye's, and on his head was a lampshade with tassels hanging down. A talking balloon came out his mouth. Jim couldn't read what she'd written in it, but he guessed 'Mr Tassel'. He guffawed silently and she leaned towards him. 'I'm Kit,' she whispered, offering him a mint.

His mam said Purgatory was a waiting room, where souls howled for years remembering their evil deeds. School was worse. He could not follow the lessons, but he followed the movements from class to class, pretending he was the Invisible Man. He sat near the window in Geography and followed the lawn-mowing sound out on the field. In Maths he followed a line of stickmen scratched on to his wooden desktop, marching up to an old inkwell. He imagined them falling in and drowning, one after another. Between classes he followed the corridors, trying to ignore the way older crowds jostled him. If he passed the younger ones, they parted before him like the Red Sea as if he were a walking curse. He followed his fate to the next classroom, thinking of when he might go home.

'It's the tinker-stinker,' he heard them say.

Time was like his da's old accordion. When you wanted to spin it out it squashed up into a dashing quickstep. When you wanted it to pass, it stretched out into a long tuneless whine.

He came across Declan in the break.

'How's it going?' said Jim.

'I couldn't do the spelling test. I handed mine in with nothing on it.'

'They made me write out a hundred lines once at the last place,' Jim said. 'I just handed in rows of waves and loops. And you know what?'

'What?'

'Nobody said anything. Perhaps *they* can't tell the difference either.'

The first fight happened near the fish and chip shop by the pier after school. There were three of them, slouching across the pavement barring his way.

'It's the Jiminy Cricket,' said one.

'Dirty Gyp,' said another.

'Hand it over,' said the third. 'We know you pinched it. My new CD.' Jim recognized him from class, a strapping boy with thick lips and pimples, and he knew it was no use saying he knew nothing. They made a grab at his sleeve.

'You pass it over – or else.'

They jumped him, he dodged, then they were all rolling on the ground, kicking and punching, a mess of sweating armpits and flailing legs, and he wished he was the camp dog Towser, so that he could give them a good bite where they'd remember. His jacket was pulled open, they yanked back his shoulder. His head hit the kerb, a knee jammed his rib.

'Stop that!' someone shouted. They froze. His three tormentors picked themselves up. It was the chippie, who'd come out, waving his fist.

'You're a desperate pack, the lot of you. Git on with you.'

'Mr Kelly,' the third one said. 'We were only after something this tinker pinched.'

'And did you find it?'

'No – but –'

'Well, off so, or I'll call the *garda*.'

They straggled away. Jim slowly got to his feet.

'Are yous alright?' said the chippie.

'S'pose.'

'D'you want some chips?'

'That Cunningham lad's always causing trouble,' the chippie said as the chips fizzled in their frying basket. 'Like his drunken tyke of a father before him. The others are just his rag-tag-and-bobtails. There's good, middling and bad Buffers – but he's bad.'

Jim started. 'Buffers? So you're one of us?'

'Aye, lad. I was a Traveller once. Still am in my blood. I settled in Dundray as a young man when I found my Eileen. The best of Buffers, my Eileen. Bought a van and mooched a living from the burgers. Then we married and I got this shop. Here's your chips.'

Jim poured the ketchup on. 'Don't you miss it?' he said. 'The travelling life?'

'What? The road, the backchat, the camp fires? Sometimes. But when it rains – then no, I'd as lief be here indoors, toasting my toes.'

The door burst open and Kit came in, breathless.

'They're after you! Moss Cunningham and his gang.'

'Don't I know it,' said Jim. Her bunches had come down, her tie flapped over her shoulder and she looked as odd as a frog in pyjamas with her misshapen clothes and blotched skin.

'Have a chip,' he said.

Before she could accept, a crowd came in, jostling at the counter.

'It's the tinker-wop again,' said one. 'Doesn't he follow you round like a bad smell?'

'I'm away,' Jim muttered.

But Kit followed him down the pier.

'Were you really baptized six times, Jim Curran?' she called after him.

He stopped to let her catch up.

'I dunno – Mam says the priests used to slip a pound into the baby shawl after every baptism, so she took me round the churches getting me baptized at all the villages. But I think she's only codding. That's Mam. You never know when she's having a rise.'

He offered her some chips and they munched in silence.

'Do you like school?' Jim said.

'My dad says I'm thicker than the kitchen table.'

'What about your mam? What does she say?'

'She's dead. And don't be saying you're sorry.'

'I wasn't. I was only going to say, "God be Good to

41

Her". It's what we say whenever we mention the dead.'

'God be Good to Her,' said Kit, trying it out. 'Are you a religious people, so?'

'Mam is. She slips into the church when it's quiet, before the tea. She sits alone in a pew and communes, like.'

'Doesn't she go to mass?'

'Not her. She doesn't like the missals the Buffers hand out. She can't read, sees.'

'She can't read?'

'No.'

'Not a word?'

'No.'

They reached the end of the pier.

'My dad's never out of church since my mam died,' said Kit. 'He does all the masses. He offers up ten novenas and swings the incense. He collects the money. You've probably seen him down Castle Street. Rattling his tin can.'

'*He's* your da?'

''Fraid so. Don't be going giving him anything because you know what?'

'What?'

'He keeps the lot. Stuffs it in an old kettle under his bed.'

'No!'

'He does so. And he never gives me any, the stingy devil. You see this uniform?' She plucked a fold of maroon material from her waist.

'Aye. You'd hardly miss it.'

'Three sizes too big. A right tent. He says it will do

till I leave school, it's a waste of money buying the right size.'

'He's a stingy devil, all right.'

They leaned against the rails, looking out to sea.

'Nothing between us and America,' said Kit. 'Wish I could swim across.'

'I can't either,' he said.

'You can't swim?'

'No. Read. I can't read.' He waited to see if she would be surprised. 'It's not just my mam. My da can't. My cousins can't. And nor me.' He shook his head.

'Not even a bit?'

'Not a holy notion.'

'Would you like to?'

Jim shrugged.

'I'm sure I could show you,' she coaxed.

'Never.'

'I could.'

'All right so – but don't be telling.'

There was a cave Kit knew, in the cliffs below the golf course. She said it was called Haggerty's Hellhole, but through a crack in the back was a larger chamber, like a cathedral, with pillars and arches, vaulting into darkness. It was a beautiful place, she said, made from a million years of wind and sea. They met in there after school, on Kit's shopping days. She brought along a book from her childhood about ponies and gymkhanas by somebody with hyphens in their name. He didn't like it much, but he tried to read it just to please her. She read a sentence and he read it after her. They used a torch to see the pages. But he relied more on memorizing her words as they echoed around the cave than on what he saw in the round of light.

'D'you think I'm pretty, Jim?' she'd said once.

He'd shone the torch into her eyes, running it down over her mouse-like nose and chapped lips, and switched it off.

'You're all right in the right light,' he'd said. She squealed and clouted him, he'd tickled her under her arms and they'd ended up having a short kiss in the dark under the dripping stalactites. Then she'd sang him a song, about a blacksmith who marries the wrong lassie, the one with the land and no heart. He lay against her and felt where the notes started and when she finished they kissed again.

'Where've you bin, Jimmy?' his da said when he got in, late.

'I went tramping on the cliffs,' he replied. 'I like the birds there.'

'Aye, it's that time of year,' his mam pitched in. 'The skylarks are up. You can't see them but you can hear them.'

'As long as it's only skylarks,' said his da.

By the end of three weeks, his after-school meanderings resulted in six bruises, a bad rib and a swell on the cheekbone, courtesy of the Cunningham gang, and a few common pronouns and twenty-eight kisses, courtesy of Kit. In class, Mr Tassey seemed to go along with Jim's rendering of the Invisible Man. He ignored him. At break, he joined the cousins in a schoolground corner and they swapped tales of Terror, Torture and Annihilation. May and Lil said their classes were full of gawps and goons, who kept away after they'd promised to put curses on anyone crossing their path. Declan never said much. He had the look of a pup with a sore toe pad and his spray came out every five minutes.

Moss Cunningham usually drifted over to deliver a few taunts with the rag-and-bob-tailing gang. Lil and May would close their eyes and speak the Cant, cursing them under their tongues, while Jim blew on his knuckles.

'Just you wait, Jim Curran,' said Moss. 'We'll get that CD back. You're a pack of thieving bastards.'

One of the gang, a girl, shook out her foxy hair and wrinkled her nose up. 'I've a song for you, Jim Curran,' she said.

> 'Jim Curran,
> Stinks like the Burren,
> Talks all foreign
> Brains like a moron.'

The teacher blew the whistle, which was just as well since Jim felt like splitting her lip.

'By tomorrow, or else,' said Moss Cunningham. 'If the CD's not back, you and your tinker cousins will know about it.'

'What CD?' snapped May. 'We don't even have a CD player.'

That night, his mam stepped through the string-bead curtain after he'd settled in his bunk. The beads clacked after her and she turned down the gas lamp. He could see her in the dusky light, her face worn with the day but smiling.

'How's school, Jimmy?'

'Same's ever. The pits.'

'How're the teachers?'

'Same's ever. The pit donkeys.'

'And how're the pupils?'

'The pit donkeys' monkeys.'

'S'that so, Jimmy?'

'Aye.'

'Only, I wondered. If maybe you'd a friend.'

'Why d'you say that?'

She shrugged. 'No reason. Just a notion. Have you any words of the reading picked up?'

He sat up. 'One or two. I can read what it says on Da's stout.'

'Even I know what that says.' She leaned over and whispered. 'If you learn a few words, could you ever pass them on to me?'

He stared at her and she reached out a hand to touch his head. He knew that she was blessing him, so he tried not to wriggle away. When she'd done, she left softly through the beads and he lay staring up at the fish mobiles spinning in slow motion from the ceiling. They'd made them together when he was small and they still hung over his pillow, spangling with carefree colours.

Later, he heard his mam and da talking when they thought he was asleep.

'Mirt's worried,' his da said. 'The asthma's worse.

He's not eating. Or talking. He's like a silent movie.'

'Declan was always delicate. Not like our Jim.'

'We should take them all out of that school and have done with it. Buffer schools never did us Pavees any favours.'

'I think our Jim's getting some words this time. You know that sign down by the cross? He told me what it says.'

'What?'

'Castlebar, three miles.'

'Even I knew that.'

Jim smiled and turned over, drawing the patchwork around his ears. There was something warm in his brain. The thought of Kit and the fishes and the new words was like bread rising with the yeast.

'Wisht,' was the last thing he heard his mam say. 'You'll wake that son of ours.'

'POLICE, POLICE, OPEN UP.'

He woke to thumps and trailer shudderings, dogs barking, lights flashing through the windows.

'God have mercy,' said Mam.

'It's the *garda*,' said Da. 'Won't they ever give us peace?'

Jim jumped down from his bunk and hopped into his trousers.

'They're after us this time and no messing,' he said. His da threw him a sour glance.

'Just you shut it, lad,' he said. He opened the door and roared. 'What the bloody heck –'

But they burst in, five of them, and they poked the

47

blankets and scattered the shoes and rummaged the cupboards. His mam followed them round, with the rosary in both hands, saying the Hail Marys. Perhaps because of her, they left his fish mobile alone. They upended the pots and hurled the cushions and when they had finished ransacking, they threw the loose things – brasses, lamps, chairs, pictures, tins, baskets – out on to the grass. His mam's Virgin Mary statue broke in two.

'What're yous looking for?' Jim said.

They didn't reply. They moved on through the camp like locusts, leaving piles on the verge behind them.

'Fit to burn,' said one. 'A lot of stinking crap.'

'What're yous looking for?' repeated Jim. His da and the other Pavees were a gathering of silent onlookers with grim faces. Jim wanted to scream, don't just stand there, stop them, but they stood stock still and said nothing. His da gripped Towser by the scruff of his neck. His dog snout pointed forwards, his teeth were bared. His body was a long, low growl.

'That your dog?' a policeman said.

'He's the camp dog,' Jim's da said. 'He belongs to us all.'

'Then where is it?'

'Where's what?'

The man folded his arms, tut-tutting, and shaking his head. He was plainclothes. Above a thin knotted tie, his throat bulged.

'As if you didn't know. The dog licence, of course.'

Nobody said anything. There was just a hardening silence. Towser's growling stopped.

'We'll be back,' said the plainclothes. 'In seven days. With your eviction notice. I advise you to be gone beforehand. Or we'll have you up in court.'

Jim stepped back into his trailer. His mam sat huddled on the bunk, her face immobile, the rosary hanging limp through her fingers.

'They're gone,' he said. 'It's all right, Mam.' He sat beside her.

'They came the night you were born,' she said. 'I was bent over with the pains and old Doll was with me, with the kettle of boiling water. They sent it flying and it splashed over my legs.'

She put her arm around him. 'They must have heard me yellin' the other side of County Cork, so help me God. But you came along anyhows, there was nothing to stop you. But they put me off my stride. You came along the wrong way round.'

He didn't know what to say.

'That was the end of the children,' she said. They sat together listening to the men's low voices seething outside. He saw the greyness of dawn creeping in through the crack in the door.

'Why do they hate us, Mam?' he said.

'They say we're the cursed people, son,' she said. 'They say we're from a long line of blacksmiths, the tinnies that the Romans bribed to make the three nails for the cross of Jesus.'

The next day, before classes started, the Cunningham gang turned on Kit.

'Jelly on a plate,
Jelly on a plate,
Wibble-wobble, wibble-wobble,
Jelly on a plate,'

they chanted. They had Kit in the middle of a ring-a-roses, with her tie askew and the buttons of her blouse undone. Moss Cunningham lashed her with a rope.

'Tinker-scuzz,' he said. 'That's what tinker girlfriends are, no better than muck themselves. If you don't get your boyfriend to hand over the CD, I'll tell your dad.'

Jim ran over and dived straight for Moss's legs. The two went flying, fisting and thrusting, while the others stood around. But in two shakes, the fight was over. A whistle blew. Mr Tassey appeared from nowhere. One of Moss's pimples had splatted into blood and pus, and Jim's knuckles itched for a swipe at the others.

'Yous – yous –' he hissed. Moss folded his arms, like the smug policeman from the night before. Mr Tassey seized Jim's shoulder. 'One more word,' he said. 'Cunningham. Go wipe your nose. Curran – come with me. I've seen this coming for days.'

As he was frogmarched indoors, he craned back to see Kit. She was buttoning up her shirt with small shaking hands. He recognized the white, vacant look in her face. She was the image of Declan.

They meant it as a punishment, but Jim found it the best school day ever. He was sent to the school librarian, a woman with wavy red hair called Mrs MacKenna.

'D'you know how to shelve?' she said.

'I do,' he said. 'I put up shelves for me mam last spring. Da showed me.'

Mrs MacKenna smiled. 'Not that kind of shelving.' She showed him the spine of a book and pointed out a code at the bottom. 'Fic,' she said. 'Means fiction. Made-up stories.'

'Aren't all stories made up?'

'So they are. But fiction's *more* made up. Supposedly. Fiction goes on the right, non-fiction on the left. Stick to the numbers, not the names, and you won't go far wrong.'

He trundled off, pushing the bookcase-on-wheels, and picked through the books. He knew his numbers, now, and because of Kit he half knew his letters. Mrs MacKenna didn't get in his way, and by noon he'd shelved them all. During lunch, Mrs MacKenna let him sit in the last bay where nobody could see him. The Cunningham gang came in searching, but she shooed them away. Then she gave him a book about birds in the British Isles. He turned the pages to a small brown bird sitting among the dunes. He looked at the black print beneath the picture and suddenly realized he could read it. *Skylark*.

He took a picture Kit had given him of herself and on the back he copied down the word: Skylark.

The next day, at break time, May and Lil said they were mitching off down the beach.

'Uncle Mirt says we can pack school in soon, any-ways,' said Lil.

'Where's Declan?' said Jim.

51

'Dunno.'

He saw Kit come rushing over.

'Is that the girl they say you're goin' with?' said Lil. 'She looks a right dumb-bell in those baggy clothes.'

'You belt up,' said Jim. 'Or I'll tell about the fags you stole from my da.'

May and Lil drifted away as Kit approached.

'Jimmy,' she panted. 'I overheard the gang in the cloakrooms. They're planning something for your Declan. They said something about Mrs MacKenna.'

They looked around, but there was no sign of the gang.

'Whatever it is, I'd say they're doing it now,' said Kit.

A terrible clarity unrolled in Jim's head. 'The library,' he said. 'Mrs MacKenna said she's off today. It'll be deserted.'

They ran indoors, up the stairs and in through the library's swing doors, but when they got there, all was still.

'Nothing,' said Kit.

'Shh –'

There was a rasp from the back bay. He ran forwards and found Declan, spreadeagled across the table with rope pinioning his wrists and ankles to the legs. They had stuffed a sock in his mouth. His eyes were glassy, as if he wasn't there, his cheeks were the colour of the sea on a bad day. Jim pulled out the sock and he could hardly breathe himself. He found Declan's spray in his pocket and yanked open his mouth. He squirted it in. Kit started untying him.

'Yous leave him alone,' Jim screamed, pushing her away violently. She reeled against another table. He gave another squirt on the inhaler and couldn't see whether it worked because his face was hot and his eyes filmed over. 'Yous leave him,' he wailed. 'Yous keep yous dirty filthy Buffer fingers off him. Yous bastard Buffers, I'll pay you all out, yous –'

Declan rasped and writhed on the table, like a fish on the end of a line. There was a rattling in his throat as if the air was drowning him, then a terrible wheezing. A long droop of spittle came down his chin.

'Declan,' Jim called. 'Declan. Come back.'

He found his penknife and cut the cords and picked the small boy up to help him breathe. Declan retched out a mix of flem and vomit. Jim held him in his arms as his mam had held him the night before. 'Our Declan,' he kept saying. 'You're all right now.' When he looked up Kit had gone. Mr Tassey was there instead.

'Kit told me what happened,' he said. 'We've called an ambulance.'

That night, Jim looked on as the men made a fire and stood around drinking stout. Declan was safe home from hospital, asleep in the top trailer, and they spoke low, as if not to disturb him.

'That's it,' said Uncle Mirt. 'That's the last time my Declan goes near that school.'

'They've given us another eviction notice,' Da said. 'The summer's over before it's started in Dundray.'

'Let's go,' someone said.

'No,' said another. 'Let's stay.'

They talked the back-and-fores-let's-goes-let's-stays, while the moon rose over the hills into the twilight, but Jim knew how it would end. It always ended the same way.

'Our Shay got properly fixed in Inverness,' said one. 'He met a Scottish lassie on the road, and they stopped at a grand site, water on tap, and they're still there with their three wee ones.'

'They've better sites over the water.'

'Better laws too.'

Jim's mam came over and pitched in. 'You men,' she scolded. 'You're all the same. The grass is always greener. You have your hopes. So you move on. Then your hopes go. You move on again. Is it never-ending? Can't we just for once stay and fight it out?'

Jim took Towser and wandered the hillside. It grew slowly darker. It wasn't properly night until gone eleven, up north. When the first star appeared, he turned back. The men had gone inside, but his mam still stood by the embers in her tweed coat.

'The men have decided,' she said wearily. 'No more school. We're packing up tomorrow and moving on.'

'Where to?'

'East to Larne for the boat. We're leaving Ireland, son. We're crossing the water. But what good'll come of it, I don't know.'

He waited in the cave next afternoon, while they packed up the camp. Would she come, or wouldn't she? He blew brash noises from the grasses he'd picked on the clifftop, and the cave laughed them back, and

54

he thought of the skylarks he'd spotted, and wished he hadn't pushed her. *Would she or wouldn't she?*

She came in with a Coke bottle for him and a smile.

'There you are,' she said.

'There you are,' he repeated. He couldn't help grinning from ear to ear.

'We're like Romeo and Juliet,' she said.

'Romeo and Juliet?' he mimicked in a la-di-dah voice.

'We read it last term. It wasn't bad.'

'Hate that crap.'

'Their families hate each other. They marry in secret. And then they both die.'

'Sounds hilarious.'

She passed him the Coke and he opened it with his knife. They sat close together on his jacket. 'We're going, Kit,' he said. 'We're moving on. Tonight.' He took her hand. 'Across the water. They're evicting us.'

'I knew it,' she wailed. 'When you all didn't show at school – I knew it.'

He drank a little and they sat in silence. 'Sing us a song,' he said. 'One last time.'

Her voice, a pure and lovely thing, filled the vast space. The notes knocked around the walls, colliding together. She sang the school hymn, but in the cathedral chamber it sounded magnificent, with the Love Divine coming up, down and around and landing in his Pavee soul.

'What's it really like being a Traveller, Jim?' she said afterwards.

He thought for a moment. 'Da says it's like being a

fox instead of a dog,' he said. 'You Buffers are the dogs, well-fed, well-trained, and we're the roving foxes, lean and free.'

'D'you like it?'

'Dunno. I just like being me.'

He offered her a swig of Coke.

'My da,' he said, 'used tell me about this old black-and-white film, with the two tramps, Stan and Ollie their names were, and they're in France, sees, and the fat one, Ollie, loves a girl who just laughs at him so he decides to drown himself. He goes off down the river to throw himself in. But he brings the skinny one with him, ties them together with rope, so's they can jump together, but before they jump the skinny one says, Do you believe in reincarnation? And Ollie says, Why yes, I do. The skinny one asks, What would you like to come back as? A horse, says Ollie, and what about you? And you know what Stan says?'

'What?'

'Stan says, "Gee, Ollie, I'd like to come back as me. I've had a swell time being me."'

'What happens then?' said Kit. 'Do they drown?'

'Nah. They jump in, but the water only reaches their knees.'

The words of his story settled back into the dark places of the cave and he could feel Kit was crying, not laughing.

'Oh, Jim,' she blurted. 'I'll miss you when you go. I don't have a swell time being me.'

'That's not true, Kit. Every time you sing you have a great time. I can see it in your eyes.'

He leaned over and blew into her face. Her feather-duster fringe rose softly. He put her small hand under his armpit to keep it warm. He turned off the torch and they lay in the dark listening to the strange sound of the surf outside.

'The tide's coming in,' she said. 'Our clothes will be ruined.'

'We could wait. Wait to see if we'd drown. Like Stan and Ollie.'

'Never.'

'We might.'

'And would you be reincarnated? And come back as yourself?'

'Maybe. But I wouldn't mind being a nice dog, whatever Da says. Running around after the sheep, the boss of the farm. Chasing car tyres, getting my strokes at night. What would you come back as?'

'Dunno. Not me. Not a dog. Maybe as my mam.'

'Your mam?'

'She was pretty. And funny. I'd come back as my mam but knowing not to marry my dad. I'd have a whole other life.'

'When you're reincarnated you forget everything. You'd probably marry your da all over again.'

'I wouldn't!'

'You would so.' He tickled her until she screeched.

'It would be nice in a way,' she said after he stopped. 'To stay here. Fall asleep maybe. And drown.'

'We wouldn't though. The sea doesn't come in this far. We'd be like Stan and Ollie. Two damp squibs.'

They lay for a while longer, but his da's accordion

must have been quickstepping again because when Kit looked at her watch she leaped up.

'My dad'll be frantic for his supper.'

Outside, the evening was clear and quiet. Before they parted she flung the empty Coke bottle out into the bright water.

'It will come back one day,' she said. 'Probably when we're so old we'll have forgotten it.'

'I won't forget.'

'Nor me,' said Kit.

He took from his pocket a stone, black and round like a glossy egg, which he'd chosen for her on the beach. 'It's yours,' he said. 'A real Dundray beauty.'

She pressed it up to her cheek, and before she could say anything, he sprinted off along the beach towards the town. Halfway to the pier he slowed to look back. He could see her, silhouetted against the fine sky, not having moved from where he had said goodbye. 'Goodbye,' he said again in his head. He waved. Maybe she could still see him, maybe not, but even when he turned away, he could still see her. He walked slowly back up to the camp, where all their Dundray life was being folded away into the trailers, and where the road beckoned again, the road from their troubles, down to the cross, up through the mountains, over to the other side of Ireland and on to more troubles, the road to Larne with its ferries sailing off to another country.

'Thought you weren't coming,' Da said. 'Where've you bin?'

'Never mind our Jim,' Mam said, throwing the

wink. 'If I know him, he was away over the cliffs, saying goodbye to his skylarks.'

'The Pavee and the Buffer' is Siobhan Dowd's first published fiction. She studied how racism affects the lives of Travellers and Roma (Gypsies) as part of her MA and in 1998 co-edited Roads of the Roma, *an anthology of Romany poetry from around the world (University of Hertfordshire Press). She was born and bred in South London, to Irish parents, and directs English PEN's literacy programme, Readers & Writers.*

The Domestic

by Allan Baillie

A story set in mid-nineteenth-century Sydney, Australia

Sophie opened her door at Balmain, Sydney, with a quill pen in her teeth on a September day of 1863. She said, 'Yuwanlinda?' to the young woman on the step.

The woman smiled and said, 'I think so.'

Sophie glanced at the woman's plain charcoal dress and the small hat and rejected the smile. She pulled the pen away from her mouth. 'Yes?'

The smile faded. 'I'm looking for work . . .'

'Oh.' Sophie looked at the woman's face – sun-touched cheeks, lips hinting a smile and still brown eyes – and turned away.

She wants to work *here*, Sophie thought. No, she can't. You know what will happen. You would have *two* nagging aunts chasing you all the time. This one would echo Aunt Linda and then have a go at you by herself.

'I don't know, it's a bad time now,' Sophie said.

'Perhaps I should see your mother.'

'My mother is dead,' Sophie snipped. No, that was stupid, she thought. You've given her the open door.

'I'm sorry. But possibly I can help your father, aunt . . .' Then the woman tilted her head. 'No, you don't like the idea. All right.' And she turned away from the door.

God, she's going, really. Sophie stared at the retreating back of the woman in stark amazement. She had never seen any adult change anything from something she had said. Until now. She lifted her hand in uncertainty.

'Who's there, Sophie?' Aunt Linda called from the shadows.

The woman hesitated.

'Wait, wait.' Sophie called after her then turned. 'Someone wants work.' Nothing you can do, she thought.

Aunt Linda pushed past Sophie and almost glared at the woman, inspecting her face and the clothes.

Sophie also looked at the clothes, seeing that they had been carefully washed and ironed but the woman couldn't hide the patches and frayed edges. Aunt Linda would see that.

'Hello, ma'am.' The woman was clutching her gloved hands. 'I was wondering –'

'Domestic,' said Aunt Linda, measuring her by the clothes and the face.

'I can do anything. Chop wood, cook, I can help your daughter with her schoolwork. I have been at a Sydney school . . .'

'School?'

'Oh yes, I can read, write, do arithmetic and I've even acted in *Macbeth* . . .'

Aunt Linda frowned. 'But why?'

'Ah . . .?'

'What's the point?'

'I'm sorry, I don't understand.'

'You are a darkie.'

The woman stood on the step in silence for a long moment.

Sophie stared at the woman in surprise. Yes, there was a faint touch of shadow in her face, as if a cloud had drifted over the sun. But it wasn't much.

'Yes,' the woman said flatly.

'A waste of time in a school. Domestic,' said Aunt Linda firmly. 'All right, I can use you. This is a big house, too much for me. You clean, wash, cook and anything I think of, but missy – what's your name?'

'Mary Ann –'

'Mary. That's enough. But if things go missing you will be dragged away by the police. Understand?'

Mary's top lip flickered, but she nodded.

'Good, just so we can understand each other. Come in, I'll show you your room.' Aunt Linda turned away.

But Mary remained outside.

Aunt Linda stopped. 'Well?'

'I have a child . . .'

Aunt Linda sighed for a long moment. 'You want to have it here? All right, all right. Just keep it quiet. Very quiet.'

'You'll never hear her.'

★

Mary moved in that afternoon with the little girl, and Sophie just waited for trouble to start. The third day there was trouble, bad trouble, but it wasn't how she had expected.

The little girl had disappeared into her room, so quiet that Sophie wasn't quite sure that she was there. Mary had been bustling around the house before sunrise and way after sunset. Sophie glimpsed her polishing knobs, dusting tables, washing clothes, sheets, scrubbing the floor, and always blindly following Aunt Linda's orders. Sophie heard her murmured words, 'Oh yes,' 'I'm sorry about that,' 'Yes, immediately,' 'Yes, ma'am', and knew that she would always follow Auntie in any argument. She was Auntie's yes-woman. But she never tried to join Auntie's constant chipping at Sophie.

At least that was something, Sophie thought.

On the third day Aunt Linda's sister Grace, who lived in the bush, dropped in for a quick visit. Sophie was pulled from her room as Mary was serving scones and tea. It began pleasantly enough with Grace nattering away . . .

'You must come up, the coaches are about as comfortable as a barrel rolling down a hill, but never mind. But the troubles we have, those damn birds, trees of galahs shrieking every day and kangaroos? You haven't seen them like this, it's a plague. You shoot one and it looks like the entire country is moving. And then there are the blacks – they are worse than the thieving galahs . . . What, oh your domestic? Never mind, they know what we think of them . . .'

Just then Aunt Linda caught the black smudge on

Sophie's right hand. She clamped her thin fingers around Sophie's wrist and twisted to see the black on her palm. 'You were supposed to be doing schoolwork, not playing!'

'It's not playing!'

'Don't shout at me, young lady!'

'Now, then . . .' Grace was leaning forwards and trying to smile.

'You have wasted another day, haven't you?' Aunt Linda's face reddened as she reeled from her chair and strode from the room.

'But . . .' Sophie looked around helplessly, at Grace with her smile fading, at the domestic frozen still with a plate of cakes, and found no help.

Aunt Linda boiled back into the room, flinging sheets of paper at Sophie. They cascaded around her, charcoal sketches of a bird nibbling a seed, a banksia seed pod looking like a withered witch, a flower drooping in the heat. 'See, Grace, what I have to put up with?' Aunt Linda sounded wounded.

Sophie scrambled after the sketches. 'They're mine! You leave them alone!'

'They are rubbish! All that money I've spent for your education, and this is how you pay me back . . .'

'They are *not* rubbish . . .' Sophie turned desperately to Grace.

'They're nice, dear, but no proper lady fiddles with art. It is messy and ugly. It is a man's job. A girl doing artwork is almost as silly as a woman writing a novel. You do some crochet work instead. Now that is a nice hobby –'

'Hobby!' Sophie reared from the sketches, shouting.

Then Mary dropped the plate.

Sophie stared at the crumbled cakes scattered on the polished wooden floor. When she saw the plate broken at Mary's feet her anger died.

Aunt Linda shook with fury. 'You stupid darkie woman! Look at what you've done!'

'Sorry, sorry, ma'am . . .' Mary dropped to a squat and began to gather up the mess.

'What do you expect from a boong?' Grace said and nudged her with a foot.

'You are going to pay for that, missy . . .'

Sophie quietly picked up her sketches and for a moment she caught Mary's eyes. But nothing was said and Sophie slipped away. She could hear the shouting echoing through the house until it slowly died.

The next day Sophie found Mary in the sunroom with her little girl. They had found her father's spyglass and the little girl was squinting at Cockatoo Island, a harsh prison and shipbuilders, half a mile from Balmain shore.

'I just was cleaning it . . .' Mary said, moving to take the spyglass from the girl.

Sophie shook her head, 'No, it's all right, and Mary – I can't remember the rest of your name . . .'

'Mary Ann.'

'Thank you, Mary Ann.'

'What for?'

'For dropping that plate.'

Mary Ann hesitated, as if she was about to say it

was an accident, but then smiled. 'I couldn't think of anything else.'

'That saved me. I would have said a lot of terrible things. How could she call my stuff rubbish?'

'She's wrong.'

A slow smile crept over Sophie's face. 'You think?'

'Yes.'

The little girl looked away from the spyglass. 'Mum says you can draw.'

'Sort of.'

The little girl nodded solemnly. 'Can I see them? I can draw too.'

'Marina, leave Sophie alone,' Mary Ann said.

'No, it's all right.' Sophie ran to her room and brought some of the sketches. 'After all, we are both artists,' she said to Marina with a spreading smile.

Marina said, 'Ooh, ah,' and used the spyglass on them.

Mary Ann looked over Marina's head. 'Yes, they are good, with only a burnt stick.'

'But I'm a girl, so they can't be,' Sophie muttered.

Mary Ann threw back her head and laughed.

'You can't see anything now,' Marina said and waved the spyglass around the sketches.

'Use the other side.' Sophie frowned at Mary Ann. 'What's so funny?'

'I've heard it before.' She sat down beside Sophie. 'In the station, in the school, in the bakery. Everywhere. You can't do anything good because you are a woman.'

'You too? I thought I was on my own. In school if

I say I want to ride a horse with my legs on both sides like a boy, if I want to play this new game cricket – they all laugh at me. Boys and girls! "You are a girl, so you can't, so there!"'

Mary Ann nodded. 'It's *not* quite like that for me. It is: "You can't do anything good because you are a *boong* woman."'

'Oh,' Sophie said clumsily. She remembered what Aunt Linda had said in the beginning.

'It is magic!' Marina skipped around the sketches, giggling and spinning the spyglass from end to end.

'That's my father's,' Sophie warned.

Marina stopped and looked around with her eyes wide. 'He's a wizard, is he?'

'No, no. He's a sailor. He's not here for months.'

'Yeah, mine's like that too. My father is not a sailor but he's gone for months and months. He's on the island –'

'Marina!' Mary Ann warned.

Marina pressed her mouth shut and looked away.

Sophie looked at Mary Ann.

But Mary Ann shook her head. 'It's nothing. Do you paint with colour?'

'Oh, I would love to paint with colour. I dream about it. But no, I don't have the money for oils. I even wanted to paint my mother when she was well –'

The front door slammed shut and Aunt Linda shouted angrily. 'Damn stupid ass! Where are you, you lazy bag of rubbish?'

'Coming, ma'am!' Mary Ann turned to Marina and told her to put the spyglass in the study and disappear with fast hand signs. Then she moved towards the shouting.

'Mary Ann . . .' Sophie whispered after her. 'How do you put up with that?'

She flickered a smile at Sophie. 'It's worth it.'

'How can *anything* be worth that?'

But Mary Ann hurried away.

Two days later Sophie found an old cigar box on her dressing table. She opened the box and found a few flat cosmetic jars but they were not filled with cream and powder but with bright powdered colours – flaming red, sunset yellow, arctic blue, purple lavender. She sat on her bed, trembling for a long moment, then she crept past Aunt Linda's room to Mary Ann's door. She tapped very quietly.

Marina opened the door, standing on a chair and yawning.

'Oh, sorry, did I wake you? I'm after Mary Ann.'

Marina shook her head. 'Not here.'

'Oh, where is she?'

Marina looked at Sophie and hesitated. 'She . . . she is by the water. She is always there at night.'

'At the water's edge? But why?'

Marina pressed her lips together and would not say any more.

Sophie slipped out of the house, padded barefoot across the lawn, past the clinking banksia and into the dark shadows of the trees at the bottom of the garden. She found Mary Ann hunched before the moonlit water, staring at the skeletal buildings of Cockatoo Island.

'Hello.' Sophie slithered up to her.

'Hey, you shouldn't be here.'

'I had to thank you for those paints. How could you pay for them?'

'Cost me nothing. Those were from flowers, grinding down bark and a few rocks. My mother taught me. She taught me a lot.' Mary Ann watched a dim light on the island.

'My mother is gone. The sickness.'

'Yes, I am sorry.'

'One moment she was laughing, chasing butterflies, then she was coughing and wheezing . . . The doctor didn't help. I tried everything – soups, honey-lemon drinks, the herbs – everything.' Sophie stared at the water. 'I felt that it was my fault, and then I was angry at her for leaving me. Crazy girl.'

'Blame doesn't fix it.'

'I know, I know, but I wish that I could blame everything on Aunt Linda. She has moved into our house because father is away sailing ships and I would be all on my own. I wish that I was on my own.'

'Just hang on. Things will change.'

'What about your father?' Sophie pictured a tall man with a tangled beard, scars on his chest and a long spear.

'Well, he's stocky, bearded, he's quite an important man around Gloucester, leads about forty shepherds, and he is white.'

'Ah.' Sophie smiled, as some of Mary Ann's puzzles clicked together.

'That's why I went to school in Sydney, learning reading, writing, arithmetic – all the things that proper young girls do. But, of course I was different. I guess he didn't know how it would be.'

Sophie watched Mary Ann stabbing a thin piece of metal into the ground.

'Some of the teachers were like Aunt Linda: "Waste of time to teach arithmetic to a boong, they can't even understand it." And the girls weren't any better: "You can come to my husband's house, Mary, any time – scrubbing the floor." It was the same in the cattle stations, the bakery, the towns. Everywhere.'

'Sorry,' said Sophie awkwardly.

Mary Ann stopped stabbing the earth and looked at Sophie in surprise. 'What, you're apologizing for Linda? They are everywhere. Everywhere. My mother met my father when he was looking after sheep near the tribe. The tribal elders were so angry about her seeing a white man that *they* tried to spear him as he slept.'

She cleaned the piece of metal with her thumb and stared at the dark island. 'Mother heard the elders and ran to tell him. So he became my father. She said you have to try to save a good one, because there are so few of them.'

A fish splashed in the dark water.

'Maybe there's a shark down there,' Sophie muttered.

Mary Ann looked sharply at her. 'You've seen them?'

Sophie shook her head. 'You hear about them.'

Mary Ann pointed the piece of metal at the dark buildings on the island. 'You know about that?'

'Cockatoo Island? It is a horrible prison. They sleep on top of each other and they have a dungeon for the worst convict – a black hole cut down in the rock. The worst prison in the continent for the worst –' Sophie swallowed. 'Marina said that her father was there.'

Mary Ann nodded. 'Fred, my husband, Marina's father, is there.'

'So that's why you're here. To watch the place where he is locked up.' Sophie thought that was unbearably sad.

'Well, no . . .' Mary Ann studied Sophie's face then she opened her hand.

Sophie breathed in. The piece of metal in her hand was a file. 'Oh.'

'Fred once stole horses and that got him to Cockatoo for the first time, but he had finished with stealing when we got married. We were settling down in Dungog – a man with a wife and child. Why would he steal horses again? He borrowed a horse – borrowed – but it was enough. They just couldn't get over a white man with a black woman. I went with Fred because *he* doesn't see the colour in my face, he just listens to what I say in my schoolgirl voice. Like I don't see *his* colour.'

'He sounds nice.'

'Most of the time. He sings a lot and he's not too bad. But – that dungeon you talked about? They put him down there for a week when he tried to escape.'

'They say it's impossible to escape.'

Mary Ann pressed her lips together. 'Maybe.' She rocked to her feet. 'You know, I think those sharks are nimbins, little monsters to frighten small children. Well, we'll find out, won't we?'

'What are you doing?' Sophie hissed in horror.

Mary Ann was dragging off her smock.

Sophie realized what she was doing. 'No, you can't!'

Mary Ann kicked her shoes off. 'You better go back in the house, Sophie. I'll see you in the morning.'

'It's –'

Mary Ann dived into the black water, surfacing a long way out before swimming towards the island.

'It's at least half a mile . . .' Sophie said dully.

She tried to watch her head moving through the dark black waters but the low chopping waves shrouded her. Soon she could not see any glimpse of her, leaving her with an empty black sea and a dull fortress on the island winking a few faint lights. She finally trod heavily to her bed, trying to stay awake until she could hear her return.

But she woke to Mary Ann calling her for breakfast.

Sophie sat at her bowl of porridge and watched Mary Ann carrying a jug with steaming milk and the teapot. She wasn't looking tired as she sashayed around Aunt Linda and the table. As if she had never dived into the shark-infested Sydney Harbour in the middle of the night to the deadly prison island. As if nothing had happened.

But Mary Ann was winking at her.

Sophie had to ask, even with Aunt Linda here. 'Um, is it a good day, Mary Ann?'

'A very good day, Sophie.'

Aunt Linda snorted. 'What's wrong with you, girl? It's a grey day and it's going to pour.'

'Still.' Mary Ann shrugged.

72

Sophie hissed softly over her porridge. That meant Mary Ann had made it to the island. Not only that, she had sneaked around the guards and – somehow – she had found her Fred in a locked building and got her file to him. *Then* she swam back again, never mind about the sharks, the cold and chop and the currents. How did she find this house at night? Doesn't matter, she did it.

That meant that the escape was underway. Nobody had got away from Cockatoo Island before, Sophie thought. But there was no Mary Ann before . . .

For the rest of the day Sophie walked with tension in her legs and arms. She rolled a pencil constantly around her palms, as she furtively glanced at the island. But nothing had happened.

Well, that's it, she thought. Fred was caught filing his leg-irons and we'll never hear about it. Except that Mary Ann doesn't seem to be worried about that.

Sophie moved closer to Mary Ann as she cooked the dinner. 'Couldn't see anything . . .'

'Wait. Wait.'

On the next day Sophie was jerked awake from a deep sleep by men shouting on the water. She slid from the bed to her window and saw several rowboats zigzagged across the harbour between Cockatoo Island and the shore.

Sophie swallowed. Fred was out!

Before breakfast a slightly annoyed policeman knocked at the door. 'Good morning, madam,' he said to Aunt Linda. 'Have you seen any strangers this morning?'

Aunt Linda squinted at him. 'No, why?'

The policeman shook his head. 'Those damn guards, they ought to be locked up with the convicts. They couldn't look after a jar of bluebottle flies.'

'The prison, is it?'

'Two prisoners escaped from Cockatoo Island last night.'

Two! Sophie's eyes widened. This was getting big.

'Cockatoo Island, where nobody can ever escape?' Aunt Linda said.

'They will be shivering. They left all their clothes on the island with their cut leg-irons.

'Naked thieves!'

'Don't worry, madam. *We* will catch them by the morning.' He tramped into the garden with two other policemen, looking for footprints.

'Bet they won't,' muttered Mary Ann softly.

Aunt Linda glared at her. 'A little bit of respect, thank you.' She fetched an old sword from the study to the breakfast table. 'I'm not going to take any chances. No stinking convict is going to get into my house!'

Mary Ann glanced at Sophie but said nothing.

Most of the day police trampled up and down on the foreshore, while soldiers blocked every street that led from Balmain. Sophie went with Mary Ann to pick up some groceries at the shops on the top of the hill and found three soldiers had stopped a farmer on a hay cart. Two privates were poking at the hay with their bayonets while a sergeant was interrogating the farmer in deep suspicion.

It's a rat trap, Sophie thought. They have no hope, now. But, but . . .

Mary Ann smiled at the soldiers as she walked into the shop. She stayed in the shop for long enough to pick up some flour, tea and lamb and for the soldiers to finish with the farmer. Then she strolled from the shop to the muttering farmer.

Sophie realized that she was not worried. At all.

Mary Ann spoke to him quickly before Sophie joined them.

The farmer looked surprised for a moment, then he shrugged and said, 'Why not?'

She smiled. 'I will see you this afternoon.' And walked away towards the house.

Sophie scowled at Mary Ann. 'What's all that about?'

'You don't want to know.'

'Hey, this is me!' Sophie protested. 'I know everything now. Almost.'

Mary Ann nodded. 'I am borrowing that cart and the old horse for a day. It will cost, but it's worth it. That's it.'

'Um, all right.' Sophie frowned.

'Can you get me an old dress without Aunt Linda knowing?'

'It's easy. There are trunks in the attic that she hasn't even opened yet. For you?'

'Not really.'

Sophie thought a bit. 'For Fred?'

Mary Ann nodded. 'Well, I've got Fred's clothes, but he will probably give them to the other man and take the dress. Fred can act if he wants to.'

Sophie slowly smiled as she worked out things. 'And the cart is for them.'

'Enough, enough.'

'But where are they? The police and soldiers are crawling everywhere.'

'Yes . . .' Mary Ann hesitated.

'You know.'

'Yes. They're where they won't look.' Mary Ann stopped on the hill and pointed at Cockatoo Island.

'They are *still* there!'

'In a disused boiler from one of the steamships.'

'But what about the clothes . . .'

'They left them so the guards would think that they swam last night and would look here for them today. Tomorrow they will hunt for them further away, but Fred and his mate will come over tonight.'

Sophie looked at the grey buildings on the island and the wind–combed water. 'Tonight . . .'

In the evening Sophie crept from her room, carrying an old dress and a bonnet from Aunt Linda's trunk. She moved across the quiet garden towards a kerosene lamp glimmering at the waterfront. Near the lamp, with a pile of old men's clothes, were Mary Ann and Marina.

'She had to see him,' Mary Ann said quietly. 'Who knows when she'll see him again?'

Marina beamed at her. 'I'm going to see Dad first!'

Sophie piled the clothes on top of the others and sat down next to Mary Ann. 'It's still,' she said. The breeze was gone now and the moon shimmered across the water.

'Too still,' murmured Mary Ann. 'Maybe the police can see a swimmer splashing.'

'No, no.' Marina shook her head furiously. 'Dad is smarter than them. He will come. You'll see.'

Mary Ann squeezed her shoulders. 'Sure.'

'I . . .' Sophie hesitated. She remembered Aunt Linda waving the old sword – funny then but it wasn't quite so funny now.

She *is* your aunt, Sophie thought. Hey, maybe she was right with the sword. And *you* are helping two convicts to escape? You don't know what they are, could be murderers, cannibals, anything. And they are coming across that water now . . . You should be telling Aunt Linda about them right now!

Sophie looked across at Mary Ann, resting her arm on Marina's shoulder. No, she thought. Mary Ann is my friend. Aunt Linda, Grace and all the others, they're pushing us down all the time. And it's *us*: What do you expect from a boong? No proper lady fiddles with art . . .

Sophie smiled at Marina. 'I want to see them coming out of the water, too. I wish I could paint it.'

'You can,' Mary Ann said. 'You'll see it, just remember.'

'I want to. I want to paint. I want to paint generals and get paid. I want to paint ships, Sydney Town, Cleopatra on the Nile. I want . . . I want to paint two bare men coming out of the water, like new animals reaching a new land, but . . .' Sophie pictured Aunt Linda and Grace seeing that painting and shuddered.

'Too hard?'

Sophie slowly nodded. 'That's the trouble with dreaming. It's only a dream.'

'I guess so.'

'Did you have one?'

Mary Ann shrugged. 'Not really. Maybe I thought of bringing up the kids in a bush town with Fred being a horse trainer. But that was plain stupid. Too many claws dragging you down . . .'

She looked across to the glimmering prison and suddenly laughed. 'I do have a little dream. I would like to be a bushranger.'

'A *bushranger*!'

'Just for a bit. Just to see Aunt Linda, Grace and the other sneering women change. And with those fat magistrates, station managers, teachers . . . Watching their faces as they try to work it out. A bushranger is holding me up, better be very polite, yes sir, here's my wallet, would you like my watch? – but hold it, it's a woman bushranger. A *boong* woman! It can't be! What do I do now?'

Sophie giggled. 'Be very respectful.'

'At last.'

They sat together in silence for a long moment, staring at the motionless water.

Then Marina jumped to her feet and pointed into the dark. 'There they are!'

Sophie peered into the night but she couldn't see anything. Her hands clamped together and she realized that she was frightened. That she should not be here.

Mary Ann stood up and waved the lantern about.

Two shadows slid from the blackness.

'Is that you, love?' A man called softly from the water.

'About time, Fred.' Mary Ann's voice was slightly shaking.

'Who's that?'

Mary Ann put her hand on Sophie's knee. 'It's all right. She's helping.'

'All right.' Fred rose from the water and Marina splashed to him. 'Hi, kid.' He scooped her from the water and put her on his shoulders. Mary Ann grabbed him as he stepped out on to the shore and crushed him to her. 'I didn't think we'd do it.'

The second man in the water looked as if he was thinking of swimming back to the island.

Fred saw his hesitation and turned to Sophie.

'Sorry, miss. About the way we look.'

Sophie felt her cheeks burning, but she shrugged.

'Well, all right, get respectable!' Mary Ann threw the dress to Fred, who put Marina on the ground.

The second man grabbed the other clothes and quickly hauled them on with a shiver.

'That was icebergs. No sharks because it was too bloody cold –'

'Brit . . .' Fred called sharply. 'There are ladies here.'

'But it was cold.'

Fred nodded at the island. 'Well, I'm never going back. No matter what.'

Mary Ann straightened the dress on Fred. 'Well, you're not there now.'

'Right. How do I look?'

'You're gorgeous, mate.' Brit snorted as he pulled on Fred's old clothes.

'The beard has to go.' Mary Ann passed a razor and soap to him.

Fred sighed as he crouched before the lapping water and attacked his tangled black beard. When he was finished Mary Ann led them quietly past the house and to the street.

Brit pressed his body against the hedge as he sucked air between his teeth.

'I don't like it. It's too quiet.'

'It's all right, Brit. They've all gone to look for us in Parramatta,' Fred said.

Brit shook his head. 'Don't like it.'

Mary Ann turned to Sophie. 'Could you walk ahead and see how things are?'

'I'll go with Soph . . .' Marina grabbed her hand and pulled her along.

Sophie squeezed her hand as they moved into the shadowy street. Now, she thought, she's protecting me.

'Do you like my dad?'

'He's got a nice smile.'

Marina sighed. 'He looks better with the beard.'

'Shh . . .'

Their footsteps echoed over the cobbles as Sophie's eyes flicked around her. A fragment of a dark shadow broke away near them and skidded across the road. She sucked in a sharp breath, but it was nothing but a black cat. The street, the block, the whole of Balmain was sleeping around them. They reached the small paddock, saw the horse and the cart and turned back.

Mary Ann was walking up the road, linked to the two men by their elbows. Fred seemed to be humming.

Brit still looked nervous but he was trying to hold a smile.

'We didn't see anyone,' Sophie said.

'What about the horse and the cart?'

'Oh, yes. *They* are up there,' Marina said.

Mary Ann's face relaxed but suddenly Brit hurried her on, as if he was seeing the end of a long race. Fred went into the paddock, running his hands over the horse before taking it towards the cart.

'It's not the best,' Mary Ann admitted.

'It'll do to get out of Sydney. Then we will get some real horses. Thoroughbreds.'

They strapped the horse up to the cart, and the men climbed on. Brit took up the reins and Fred put on the bonnet.

'Well . . .' Mary Ann stepped back.

'Aren't you coming?' Fred sounded surprised.

'I was going to stay on for a bit. The woman owes me some money.'

'Don't be daft. We'll get money on the road.'

'What are you going to do?'

Fred shrugged. 'I got no choice. They're going to hunt me now. I have to be a bushranger. All right?' He reached out for Mary Ann.

'Well . . .' She considered his hand, then looked at Sophie's face. 'Linda won't give me my money, will she?'

Sophie's eyes shifted away as she realized what was about to happen. 'I don't –'

Mary Ann shrugged. 'There's the plate and she'll find other things. She is going to cheat. They always do.'

Sophie swallowed. 'Yes, yes, Aunt Linda will keep everything. She'll charge you for the plate, the food you ate, the rent for your room. Go.'

Mary Ann nodded, then swung Marina up to Fred and leaped after her.

Sophie stood beside the paddock gate, watching the cart rock down the lonely street, and felt strangely hollow.

Then the cart stopped, Mary Ann leaped down to the cobbles and ran up to Sophie. She grabbed her shoulders, kissed her and then suddenly shook her fiercely. 'Don't let it go. Ever!'

She hurried back to the cart.

Sophie was serving tea for Aunt Linda and Grace on a late winter afternoon.

'It is terrible now,' Grace sighed and clinked her cup. 'You can't take a coach out of town without being robbed by bushrangers. The papers say that Thunderbolt has claimed the highways.'

'Terrible,' said Aunt Linda.

'Have you seen him?' Sophie said.

'Seen him! My girl, I have been bailed up by him. And worse with his damn darkie woman.'

'A woman? Can't be.' Aunt shook her head.

'Oh yes, definitely. Maybe she's your runaway, but who remembers their faces. They call her Princess Yellow Long – she's tall and she's got a light colour. She doesn't have a gun but she gets all the jewellery from the ladies – even the hidden jewellery . . .'

'Shocking. What is this country becoming? What

are *you* leering about?' Aunt Linda snarled at Sophie.

'Nothing, nothing.' Sophie slid away from the lounge.

She went into her room and slowly spread a sheet of blank paper on her table. For the first time in a long time she took the cigar box and began to open the small jars, filling her room with the touch of crushed herbs, flowers and sandstone.

And began to paint.

Allan Baillie was born in Scotland but has lived in Australia since he was seven. He is a full-time writer and many of his novels have received awards, including Adrift, Little Brother *and* China Coin. *Allan Baillie is married to a Chinese-Australian and they have a daughter and a son.*

The Great Satan

by Farrukh Dhondy

A story set in present-day East London, England

Hate my name.

'Asthma? But that's a disease!'

'A–S–M–A' – but they didn't want to know and I didn't want to say it as my mum and dad say it because it becomes worse. The A–S sounds like the bad word for backside.

I asked my mum once if I could change my name to Ally, which even sounds Muslim, but she said no and not even to mention it to Dad because he'd get wild. That was before I went to big school where nobody would know my name. There weren't any kids from my old primary school, because that was the time we shifted house. We moved from a place in London called Spitalfields to right out in Wanstead and my elder sister Razia moaned and said she wouldn't go, but she went. She didn't like the travelling but Dad said it was better for me because I'd get to go to St Kate's.

Razia's clothes are still in her room at the top of the

house in her wardrobe and I sneak in and lock the door and change into them. There's a blue silk dress with Chinese patterns in red, green and gold which is gorgeous. It has a ribbon round the neck with a bow and it's small for her and very short so it sort of fits me, except I can't fill it out in the chest because I haven't grown – you know – boobies like Razia has. If Dad catches me wearing it, then I'll get in his bad books. Except he doesn't read many books except the Koran and that's a good book. But he'll just shout mostly to himself, not at me, and sulk and go on about England spoiling young people till I want to scream.

He didn't like what she used to wear and used to say that it was very shaming and spoiling the family's name and all that, but Razia didn't care. She would always sneak out wearing a *salwar* and *khamiz* and a headscarf and whatever he wanted, and carry her real clothes in a bag and go and change in the McDonald's loo before going to town. The people there must have thought she was Superwoman – goes in wearing one thing and out wearing another. I knew because I caught her doing it once when me and my mates went in for a forbidden cheeseburger. Razia said she'd pay for the meal if I kept my mouth shut and she in turn wouldn't grass me up for eating McDonald's which wasn't *halal*. Dad would do his nut if he found out.

I wear a *chador*, the headscarf, over my head to school every day and to the mosque. Dad drives us on Fridays and Mum and I go upstairs with the women and he goes into the yard with the men. Some of the women, even the ones who are only twelve like me, wear a full ı, like black or brown all over with slits and holes to see through. We sit and listen to the sermons and my mind starts thinking weird things. Like, after one day when the whole of our year at St K's had to line up for the Christmas photograph, I was thinking what would happen in a school where all the girls have to wear the full Monty – like all of them sit covered up for the photo? Ten rows of black hoods and no one saying 'cheese'? With the big blackout in the centre on a chair – the headmistress. 'The Girls of Year Eight, Two Thousand and Whatever.'

I don't listen to the preachers before the prayers because where we are, the women can't see their faces. They are downstairs standing in front of the men and we can only hear them through a loudspeaker. I don't get what they are saying because they talk a bit of Arabic and then they talk English but I can't understand their accents. My dad and mum can and my dad even knows a bit of Arabic and keeps telling us to learn, but it's all Greek to me.

And then we pray and I think about it a lot. Everyone believes in God, even if at St Kate's it's a Christian god, who the RE teacher said was the same. She, Miss Pryce, told us that God could be called the Lord or He could be called Allah or Jehovah or Ram, because that's what different people like Christians, Muslims, Jews and Hindus call Him. Same difference. My dad said that was wrong and he got well annoyed. Not because Miss Pryce is a Christian but he said God couldn't be called Ram, because Ram was a man and the Hindus had stories about Ram and you couldn't have stories about God. I suppose he is right.

When I told Miss Pryce at school, she said the Hindus had a different idea of God and everyone must be allowed to have their own idea. I couldn't argue with that, but I know my dad would.

He's got very strict since Razia went off to Pakistan. She's a pharmacologist and she's gone to do some good in Pakistan by helping to make medicines. She always wanted to be a doctor but they didn't take her in medical school and I remember she cried a lot and I didn't know why anyone should cry when they didn't take you in school, because you could stay at home and watch telly. And Dad and Razia both said that other girls had got in to the same medical school with lower marks and it was only because Razia was not a white girl that she'd got prejudiced against. Mum said, 'When you come to a foreign country you have to be ready to bear some troubles and trials.' So Razia said it wasn't a foreign country, it was her own country but it was an unfair country and she didn't care anyway.

It was not good when we moved house. Rotherfield Row is a nice street and each house has a little front garden and a long back garden. In Spitalfields our house door was right on the street and there was no backyard or garden or nothing, but Razz said that was better because nobody could build a fence against us. As soon as we moved in, like the next day, the neighbours built a high wooden fence of tin and wood on their side of the back garden and up in the front garden. My mum just said when you move house you have to be ready to bear such tribulations. She says that in Urdu. My dad said it was good because he didn't want them looking into our back garden and seeing the women's underwear on the washing line. Razia said it was a damned cheek and she made tiger noises at the woman who lived next door when she saw her at her little front gate. The woman got startled and Razia laughed and ever since when she saw anyone from that next-door family she practised her animal noises – pigs, tigers, owls and other creatures. She didn't care if they thought she was mad – a girl with a headscarf and covered up arms and legs being savage.

In the house on the other side there's a bald man with a nearly bald wife and both of them wear round specs and are quite old and work in their garden all the time. They've got good flowers and the fence between their house and ours is all tatty and broken and worn away with rain but they don't care. They always smile and say, 'Cold, ain't it?' even if it's hot and rub their hands and their eyes twinkle. So Razz and I call them the Twinklies and the other nasties we call the Fencies.

'Very cold,' my mum used to reply to them. Even if it was hot. 'But coming in England one has to bear these things.' She shouldn't say that to them.

'Oh that's right, that's very right,' was what the old man and woman would say to any answer we gave. And Dad, whenever he saw them, would rush to say, 'Very cold today!' before they could say, 'Cold, ain't it?'

So it must have been the Fencies who spilt our

rubbish bins all over the pavement and into our front garden. My mum had to sweep it up and the other people from our street who passed stopped to say it was probably foxes. Razia was convinced it was not foxes. It was the big bad wolves, the Fencies.

Dad got very annoyed when Razia wouldn't come to the mosque with us and when she started staying out on Fridays and Saturdays even. She would phone and say she was in town with Nazrina, her friend from college, but Dad argued with her. She said he couldn't stop her because she was old enough and earning her own money and a British citizen and he said she shouldn't argue with her father, especially not in front of her younger sister. I think he loves her very much because he was very sad when she decided to go to Pakistan. Dad went to London to make all the arrangements and Mum and I went to see Mum's cousin in Leamington Spa and stayed there over the New Year. Razz said she'd write letters and she did. Mum and Dad always told me her news but they never showed me her letters even though I wrote to her saying she should write to me and not only to them. And then she did write. She just said she loved me very much and that I was to be good and listen to Mum and Dad and work hard at school and go to prayers at the mosque and say my prayers at home. She didn't say anything about Pakistan.

'Why does she write on this funny paper with lines?' I asked Mum, but Mum was blubbing about something else and didn't reply. I think she was missing Razia.

I found Dad in Razia's room, the attic room with the sloping roof, just standing and staring at the walls.

'Why didn't Razz take her clothes to Pakistan, Dad?'

'They don't wear these clothes in Pakistan, thank God. I should burn them.'

'I don't think you should, Dad, Razz will be very angry,' I said.

'What about *my* anger?' he asked but I knew he was asking the room, not me. He looked sad and he put on his furry cap and went downstairs and out of the house.

And again that night the foxes must have got at our dustbins because they tore up the black plastic bags and threw everything everywhere and made a mess in front of our house. They didn't pick on anyone else's, even though the whole street's bins were waiting patiently for the dustmen. I helped Mum clean up the mess.

'They are trying to give us a bad name in the street,' Dad said and he went and rang the Fencies' bell.

'I don't know what you doing this for,' Dad said to Mrs Fency who came out in her dressing gown.

'What the hell are you talking about? Get off my doorstep,' Mrs Fency shouted and Dad rushed at her bins to get his revenge on them and dragged the black plastic bags out and jumped on them.

'I will show you what I am talking about,' Dad shouted. 'You sneaking and slying in the night on my bins.' The black plastic burst as he jumped on it.

Mum and I were in the front garden and she rushed and grabbed Dad's shirt and tried to pull him away. Mr Fency and Master Fency, who was older than me but still in school, because I used to see him coming and going in a school blazer, came out with broomsticks and iron rods and hit Dad in the head and the face till he fell down.

Mr and Mrs Twinkly came out of their house and other neighbours from all sides and Mr Twinkly went and picked Dad up and that stopped the Fencies from beating him with their sticks. I wanted to scream but I didn't. Dad had two cuts on his face and Mum said he should call the police. They began to babble away in Urdu which I don't understand and then Dad said 'passport' and 'visa' in English which I did understand and Mum said 'checking' and then she mentioned Razzi twice, meaning my sister, and she hid her face in her headscarf and I knew they didn't want to have the police come in the house. But I wanted them.

'Why not call the police? They hit you,' I said.

'Just keep quiet, Asma, go to school,' Dad said.

'This is an unlucky house,' Mum said.

'Even if it is, don't bring superstition into it,' Dad said. 'We don't believe in luck.'

Mum washed his wound in hot water and put a big piece of cotton wool on the cut on his face. She put some bright yellow turmeric and other stuff from the kitchen, which she thinks are good for cuts, on the cotton wool. Yuck!

By the time I started out for school, the Fencies had cleaned up their dustbin bags and so had we and Rotherfield Row was quiet and the leaves were falling from the plane trees on each side and covered the pavements where the larger, detached houses began.

Suppose the foxes had done it?

Sometimes on the way if a passer-by stares at me because I've got a headscarf, I push it back and on to my neck, but somehow after that second fox-bin day when they beat Dad, I just wanted to keep it on, like protection, even though it was thin, transparent cloth and wouldn't protect me if someone hit me on the head. It was like wearing a mask when you didn't want to show your face, even though it didn't cover it. I can't explain but it makes me feel like when you hide under the blankets to keep the monsters out. The headscarf is very thin really and you can even see the parting of my hair through it.

That week on Friday at the mosque there were men outside handing out leaflets in Arabic, Urdu and English and Dad took one to read. Mum said a very important person had come to speak and we should listen carefully. The important man spoke in foreign and there was another person turning what he said into English every little while. So the speech took twice as long that day and because the man was important he added more time so it took three or four times as long. I hate waiting and listening to what I don't want to listen to. I didn't hear a word of it or I didn't think I did which is weird for a reason I'm going to tell you later. I was sitting on the carpets, because we all sit on the floor in the upstairs hall, and I was looking out of the carved marble patterned trellises that fill the windows. Mum told me that in Pakistan in a miracle mosque women who didn't have babies came and prayed for one and then tied a bit of wool to one spar in the marble trellis thing. And then if God gave them a baby they would come and take their own woollen thread off and praise Allah. But she said not to tell Dad because he didn't believe in these sorts of miracles. He didn't even believe we should ask God for anything.

After the prayers Dad said we should go home by bus because he was not going with us. Then at the bus stop on the Mile End Road we saw him with all the other men in their white shirts and trousers coming out of the mosque yard and shouting things and raising their fists. And policemen came and stood in rows to stop the men overflowing into the street and stopping the traffic. Which was good because they didn't stop our bus and I was dying to get home and do a wee. I don't use the mosque toilets because they stink and if I'm with Mum I can't pop into Macky D's.

'What are they shouting about?' I asked Mum.

'Sometimes to be a good Muslim it's necessary to shout,' she said.

'Like football supporters?' I said. She wouldn't know, my mum. The girls at school all support West Ham, but Mum wouldn't know West Ham from roast ham and if I mentioned it at home she would probably think I was talking about pig's meat and it wasn't *halal*.

I said I didn't listen to what the preacher was saying, but I tell a lie. It was all in my head, like the words of a song that you hear on Kiss FM twenty times a day and they get stuck in your head without your knowing that you know them. But when other girls start singing them, you can sing all of them too.

It all came pouring out two days later. I'd not

thought about it. About what the person who was turning the important man's foreign words into English was saying, and I don't even remember my dad saying much when he got back home that night. But I remember they said something about the Great Satan. And I didn't know what it was, but it was the worst thing in or out of this world. I was thinking about the Fencies being the Great Satan.

When Dad came back I remember asking him why we didn't phone Razz and why she didn't phone us from Pakistan. Other relatives used to phone from there.

'Razia is very busy,' Mum said.

'Pakistan is now asleep,' Dad said.

And I knew that both of them were making an excuse. Razz would have phoned. So why did they have to cover up the fact that she didn't? And that night I had this dream that Razz was really dead and I woke up with a scare. Then I told myself that I'd read her letters and it was her handwriting and my dad wouldn't lie, not about anything. Lying would be like a shame to the family. So maybe she wasn't dead and then I fell asleep again and dreamt she was plucking cotton in the fields in Pakistan with a basket on her back into which she was throwing the cotton as she smiled and worked. But still I prayed to God that she wasn't dead even though Dad had said it was wicked to ask Allah for things. He was not Santa Claus.

All the girls in St K's have to pass an exam to get in and they are not really posh, but they're clever and some are real smarty-pants and show-offs. Everyone is always talking about who is doing the music exams and who is cleverer than whom and their mums all think about who can act the best and sing the best and all this and who will get to university. Dad and Mum wanted me to get into this school and Razz took me for the test. I passed it and got in and Mum and Dad bought Pakistani sweets and sent some to the Twinklies next door to celebrate.

But then on my first day, in my new uniform with black tights to cover my legs because Dad insisted, the twins in my class, Carol and Kara, said I only got in because I was a Paki.

So I said, 'I'm telling,' and the twins said, 'Then you'll be a grassy Paki.' So I said I wasn't really telling but I added that I didn't really care if they were rude but they ought to because their tongues would slowly rot in their mouths.

That was a bad start but later on as the days passed I became best friends with Kara and we used to share our sandwiches because neither of us ate school dinners and she was Jewish and Dad even said it was OK to eat her food.

The day after my bad dream about Razia, Miss Pryce was talking about war being the worst thing in the world, because people who didn't know each other killed each other and she asked the class if we agreed. We all agreed, even though I was thinking it wasn't good to kill people one knew either.

'Does anyone else have any thoughts about what is right and wrong in this world?' she asked.

No one said anything and Prycey started talking

about how in some places women were not given any freedom to dress as they liked and go where they wanted. And there were some countries where girls weren't even allowed to go to school or even to go to work where there were men. I knew she meant some Muslim countries, but she didn't say it because I was in the class and I could see her looking at me to see what I was thinking.

Kara saw her looking at me and put her hand up and said she thought prejudice was wrong.

'What do you mean by that?' Miss Pryce asked.

'Like calling somebody cruel names, just because they wear headscarves, like calling them "Paki" or making fun of people because they have something wrong with their legs or hands or heads,' Kara said.

'What do you mean, their heads?' Miss Pryce asked. 'Do you mean people who are mentally ill?'

'No, miss, I saw a man with a very thin and long head like a neck on a bottle and . . .'

The class started to laugh at this because they must have imagined the bottle-head man but Kara turned on them.

'See? I stopped myself laughing – because what would you feel if you was him?'

'Were him,' Miss Pryce corrected. And when Kara didn't take any notice she said, 'Can you give us any examples of this sort of prejudice?'

'I can,' said Kara and without looking at me because I was sitting just next to her in the back row she says, 'Throwing people's dustbins on the pavement and scattering all the rubbish and pretending that the foxes did it just because they are a Pakistani family is wrong. And that's an example, miss.'

I was blushing. I wished she hadn't said that, because I'd told her what happened and now she was giving the secret away, so I pulled my headscarf over my eyes.

'Kara has a strong and, I think, correct point of view,' Miss Pryce said. 'And why are you hiding your face, Asma? Do you have something to say?'

'No, miss,' I said. I don't know what made me change my mind, but then I said, 'Yes, actually I do, miss.'

We all had to stand up when we spoke to Miss Pryce. I stood up and the words just came out of me.

'I think the way that people behave without proper laws is wrong. They kill children and abuse them and then women go around without shame showing their bodies and there are a lot of drug addicts and people who steal from old ladies and don't believe in God . . .'

I couldn't think of anything more.

'And what do you think we can do about it?' Miss Pryce asked.

'In my religion which is Islam there is no such wickedness allowed. So if everybody became a good Muslim the world can get rid of such things and shameless and cruel behaviour. And kill the Great Satan.'

I said it and sat down.

She looked at me with very wide eyes.

'That is a very strong point of view, Asma, thank you. But don't you think that you can be good without being a Muslim?'

'No,' I said.

I swear the whole class gasped. They were all looking at me. I set my mouth to look very serious and narrowed my eyes and stared back at all of them from the back row. I didn't want to say any more. Just what I had said had a strange effect. No one came to talk to me in the playground except Kara and I heard other girls from my class whispering to their friends as I passed through the corridor. Maybe they were talking about me and maybe they weren't.

'Do you really believe what you said?' Kara asked. 'And what's the Grand Satan?' She's got lovely long eyelashes and thin eyebrows which go up and down when she's talking.

'Yes, of course I believe it,' I said and pulled my head-scarf around me. 'And it's the Great Satan, not "Grand". It's all the evil things in the world put together.'

'But how is the world going to become Muslim? They might not want to. My dad wouldn't,' she said.

'You'll see,' I said. I didn't know what else to say.

'Do your mum and dad believe that?' she asked.

'Of course they do,' I said.

'And your older sister? You told me she was cool.'

'Yes,' I said. 'She is cool. And you know when Miss Pryce said that there are evil doctors all over the world who are making all sorts of germs and bombs and gases to kill people?'

'You mean the terrorists?'

'Well, I can't say exactly who, because that would be giving away a secret, but she's gone to help them. That's why she's not living with us. She was at university and she knows all about chemistry and germs and things.'

'That's horrible,' Kara said.

'Oh, she won't use them on good people. Just wicked people. The Great Satan and people like that,' I said. 'It's all very secret, but I've told you and you'd better keep it to yourself.'

Kara nodded.

But she didn't keep it secret. She told her twin sister Carol who told Abbie who told Terry and the next day two girls from the senior class came up to me. I didn't know them but they were ugly and I immediately thought they should be called Nasty One and Nasty Two.

'You! Raghead! Is your sister really a terrorist?'

'She is a scientist and nearly a doctor,' I said. 'And in this country you can believe whatever you like, right? And if she's fighting against you, I'm glad.'

'Your sister is a traitor and so are you. Do you know what that means?'

'Yes,' I said when actually I didn't.

'It means being an enemy of the Queen and all the people and they'll catch you and hang you,' said Nasty One.

I just walked away. It had nothing to do with the Queen. I hadn't brought her into the story.

'Don't lose your rag,' Nasty Two shouted behind my back.

Then the next day the Headmistress called me into her office from the playground. Miss Pryce came to fetch me. I was thinking what Nasty One had said about hanging me. She must be part of the Great Satan because she was a big stroppy girl with bushy blonde hair and little golden hairs coming out of her nose and I was going to tell on her if the Head said anything to me.

'Were you telling the truth, Asma my dear, when you spoke to some of your friends about your sister and what she is doing?' the Head asked after she'd sat me and Miss Pryce down on her sofa.

'I don't know what you mean, miss,' I said.

'That your sister has gone away to be a terrorist or train terrorists or something like that? Is she really a chemist?'

'Yes, miss,' I said. 'Why shouldn't she be?'

'Of course she should be. But do your parents know where she is and what she's doing?'

I didn't reply.

'You mustn't spread these stories. People get frightened,' the Head said. 'Unless it's true.'

'Asma doesn't tell lies,' Miss Pryce said.

'Did your sister tell you this herself? And where is she? Has she gone abroad? What you have said is very serious, you know? I must speak to your parents.'

'Can if you like,' I said.

Of course I just said that. I didn't want her to.

'I do like,' she said, cheekily. 'Will you take this note to your parents, please, Asma?'

I took the envelope she held out. The Head said, 'It only says I would really appreciate it if I could have a word with them. Now don't forget.'

I said I wouldn't and Miss Pryce came out with me into the playground.

I hated Kara for telling everyone.

'Are your friends OK with you, Asma?' Miss Pryce asked.

'Of course they are. But my only real friend is Kara and she was the one who went and told.'

'What you said is very serious and some parents have got to hear and they've complained. They think you were boasting that your sister is a terrorist. If it were anything else, it would be none of anyone's business. And . . . and we know that your parents are good people. But this is a church school and of course your parents said that they were Muslims and we were very happy to have you here, very proud. There are eight Muslim girls in the school – you know that and we are proud of you all.'

I didn't know why she was saying all that. I was worried. I had to give the note to my dad and he'd come and talk to the Head and then he'd kill me.

I didn't tell a lie. At least it didn't feel as if I'd told a lie. It felt as though it was the truth, even though I knew that Razz was making medicines to help poor people in Pakistan.

I gave the note to Dad. He looked at it and asked me why the Headmistress wanted to see him.

'How should I know?' I shrugged.

'Have you been rude or done some rascally thing?' he asked.

'No, Dad,' I said.

He came into school the next day just as we were all leaving at home time. He was wearing his tweed jacket with his green sweater under it and he had his furry cap. He smiled at me and we spoke at the gate as the other girls crowded through it.

'Is that your dad?' Kara asked as we walked out together. We used to take the same bus part of the way home.

I nodded. I didn't feel like saying anything. My heart was beating something wicked and I got a feeling as if my stomach was collapsing. The Head would tell him and how the story had spread and how some girls' parents had come in to complain about our family. And he would be furious about giving the family a bad name and about me telling people something which wasn't true. And then, even as I walked with Kara next to me rabbiting on about something, I was picturing Razz in a mask with a nozzle, working with some tubes and looking down a microscope, wearing rubber gloves and shaking her head. Had I seen her eyes in my dreams? I had seen the picture before, I was sure.

I told Kara I wasn't taking the bus and was going to walk home. She had violin lessons with Carol and so she had to rush, she said. It took me a long time walking home but I knew I'd still be there before my dad was and then I'd have to wait. I plashed through the leaves at the end of our road. They were thick on the ground just here. And where the trees stopped, the roads and pavements were bare and the houses got smaller. A man with specs was fixing a car and he cheerily said, 'Hi, there,' as I passed.

★

Mum gave me some chicken in a chapatti and some cranberry juice but I didn't feel hungry or thirsty. I said I had homework and then went from my room up to Razz's attic. I sat on her bed. The room still had posters of a black man smoking a pipe and Badly Drawn Boy who was quite nicely drawn.

I just sat there. I looked out of the window of the attic. It was grey and soon it would get dark. Then I heard Dad's footsteps and his voice asking Mum where I was. He came past my room, straight up the stairs. He turned the light on as he entered Razz's room and the sudden glare hurt my eyes so I shielded them.

'I just come from your school,' he said.

I didn't say anything. He sat on the bed next to me and took off his furry cap and rubbed his head. His hair is getting thin.

'I must to talk with you, darling child,' he said. And before I could say anything he went on. 'You see, we have been telling you lies. Your mummy and me.'

'What?' I said.

I was the one who had told the lie. And just as I was thinking that, there was a shout downstairs. It was Mum. She shouted at someone and then she screamed, some words in Urdu which I know mean 'Oh Lord!'

Dad was off faster than a bullet, down the stairs. I ran after him. Down two floors and into the hallway where Mum was still shouting. By the time I got down Dad had put out a fire by stamping on it, a burning piece of cloth which had a smell of petrol. The strip of carpet in the hall had a hole in it with the wood below still smoking and one wall had got black. Mum had a note

103

in her hand. It had come through the door first and then, she said, while she was stooping to pick it up someone threw the burning rag through the letterbox.

My dad grabbed the note. He held my mum by the arm. She was crying and for the first time I saw her bury her head in Dad's shoulder, like lovers in the films. And he was holding on to her and looking at me.

Then we waited in the hall and Dad opened the door and stepped outside. He shouted into the grey evening. Some curse in Urdu. Of course whoever had thrown the burning rag was gone. He never cursed but I knew it was bad words. He slammed the door again.

'This is not a good house,' Mum said. And again she cuddled up to him and he put his arm around her. I had never seen him do that. Mum and Dad never did that sort of thing.

'Come in the kitchen,' Dad said. Then he read the note.

'It's not the house. It's people,' he said. 'Some people. Bad people.'

'WE DON'T WANT YOUR KIND HERE' the note said. That's all.

Dad asked me to sit.

'I was telling you that we told you lies,' he said.

I thought I should be crying but I didn't feel like it. I was the one who had told lies or maybe I'd just described my dream. But I couldn't even remember if that was one of the dreams. I had told Kara what I saw in my mind and I believed it was as true as anything needs to be. Razz was working against the Great Satan and now I knew that I had got that, about the Great

Satan, from the important preacher who had spoken at the mosque when I wasn't listening. But I knew that the Great Satan, wherever he was, must be bad even though I didn't know what he was.

'I should have told you where your sister is,' Dad said.

'Razz is in Pakistan, doing good,' I said.

'No, she is not,' said Dad. 'She is in jail in the south of England because she done some bad things. She made bad drugs – all this Extra-C. Because she falled into bad company.'

I didn't tell him that he meant 'Ecstasy' which was what the big girls in school were talking about because it makes you go mad and feel good.

'And it maybe is my fault because I stop her from doing all things she liked like a modern girl.'

Jail. Razz couldn't be in jail. Not prison. This was shame. This was . . . Oh God, poor, poor, poor Razz. And then I thought, he's not telling the truth. Why? Why is he lying? I am the liar.

'No, Dad, she's in Pakistan. Razz is in Pakistan.'

'Sorry,' he said and looked at the floor. He didn't want to look into my eyes. 'She was going with bad girls and boys and making drugs for them and the po-lis come with raids in their house and capturing all of them and take her away, and she was one who was controlling chemical equipment,' Dad said.

My mum started crying silently, wiping her eyes with the corner of her headscarf.

'She will come out in three weeks and we was going to not tell you. This has shamed our family. But maybe it is my fault because I told her to be good and live with our rules but she want to live in English rules. I love Razia too much. I have gone and seen her every week but your mother could never come because she is too sad.' Then he was silent, stunned by what he had told me.

'Three weeks?' I said. 'So why did you lie?'

Dad didn't answer. Had he forgotten about what I said to Kara and what the Head told him and about the note that came through the door and the fire?

'Isn't it less shame that I said she is fighting the Great Satan than that she is in prison?' I asked.

And now I looked at Dad and his cheeks were wet too. He shook his head and the teardrops moved slowly down and spread into wetness. I had never seen him cry. He was still fumbling with the note and with his furry cap.

'I tell you why I told Kara lies about where Razz was. I can tell you,' I said and I noticed that my voice was louder than I wanted it to be and the echo went all round our house.

Dad shook his head, saying nothing, standing in the centre of the kitchen.

'I said it because I wanted to be on the right side and I wanted them to think that Razz was on the right side. Against the Great Satan.'

'That is good,' he said.

'Who is the Great Satan, Dad?'

He didn't answer straight away. He turned his furry cap in his hand.

'There is no Great Satan, my daughter,' he said in

Urdu. 'No Great Satan. Lies is the Great Satan. All lies. Only what you are afraid of, that is the Great Satan. And if you don't fear him and if you don't feed him, he is dead. My older daughter has been in jail for wrong things and is coming out after punishment and won't do wrong things again. And my younger daughter wants to be on the side of good and I love her. God bless her.'

I hugged him and my mum came over too and we hugged each other all together and I wished Razz was there and thought she will be, she will be. Soon.

Born in Poona, India, Farrukh Dhondy has lived and worked for many years in Britain as a writer and broadcaster. His books include works of fiction for teenagers, most recently the critically acclaimed Run *(Bloomsbury, 2002). He also wrote the screenplay of Dev Bengal's recent film* Split Wide Open.

Smoke

by Sean Taylor

A story set in present-day Brazil

No one else knew you could get into the side of the bridge. There wasn't any path down. The undergrowth was full of thorns. But Danilo knew the way. He dropped into the stream where it had dried up. Then he ducked through the shadows. And there it was: an opening in the concrete, big as a door.

Danilo looked about inside. The wood was propped by the wall. The tools he'd got hold of, nails, hinges. Everything was there. All he needed now was a pair of wheels. And he had to make up his mind if he was really going to do it.

Up in the house, Dad stared into the dented pot on the gas ring. He was a tall, wiry man with redness smeared into the corners of his eyes. When the water began to hiss he snapped off the gas.

'Where the hell's Danilo?' he muttered, picking up the pot by its rim. 'It's Monday for Christ's sake. He knows there's work to do.'

Four years earlier Danilo's dad had been making a reasonable living. He'd been driving freight all over Brazil – up to the north, down to the south, right over to the border with Bolivia. Then, one night, he stopped to fill up and drink a coffee about a hundred kilometres outside Rio de Janeiro. As he came back to his lorry, two men were waiting, one with a pistol, the other with a metal bar.

'Give me a chance, brothers!' he said. 'I'm only a simple man trying to make my living!'

But that was as far as he got. The gun jabbed his ribs. He dropped the keys. Moments later the two guys were off in the lorry with its cargo: 320 crates of T-shirts.

When the same thing happened to a white driver, the boss believed the driver's story. But he never believed Danilo's dad.

'You're lying through your teeth,' he said. 'You planned the whole thing with your black friends.'

He sacked him. Then he got the police involved.

Dad's eyes burned whenever he spoke about that boss of his.

'The son-of-a-bitch,' he'd hiss. 'If I'd made money from the hold-up like he said, I wouldn't have got us kicked out of the flat for not paying the rent. My wife wouldn't have run off. And Danilo and I wouldn't be doing the lousiest work anyone ever did.'

He dropped a spoonful of coffee into the pot and stirred it noisily. Then he pushed open the door.

'EH!' he yelled. 'DANILO!'

Under the bridge, Danilo had a hammer in his hand.

He was going to nail a strut of wood across a pair of planks. But when he heard his dad's voice he dropped the hammer. Then he threw the strut against the wall and kicked the planks apart.

When he appeared in the doorway, Dad was sipping his coffee.

'Where in God's name have you been?' he growled.

'I had a headache. Went up to the twenty-four-hour pharmacy for an aspirin.'

'It must be that stupid haircut gave you the headache,' said Dad. Then he coughed loudly and spat out of the window.

Danilo smirked and ran a hand over his head. On one side the hair was shaved close with a stripe down the middle. On the other side the hair was long.

'Zivanete did it for me,' he said.

'Well Zivanete should know better,' muttered Dad. 'You look like a freak.'

Danilo grinned. Dad sipped at his coffee.

'What you gawping at?' he snapped. 'You've got five minutes to shift that black arse of yours up the hill and help me make some money.'

Danilo peered at himself in the small mirror hung on the wall then went to get the forks.

The sun was low over the tower blocks as they set off up the slope. Danilo led the way, trudging through wads of soggy rubbish bags, dry coconut husks, crushed milk cartons, bones, cans. Halfway up, a dog with ragged ears came padding through the sunlight.

'Git!' said Dad, flapping the bundle of empty sacks he was carrying. The dog ignored him so Dad reached down and chucked a bottle. PASH! Splinters of glass flew in the air, and the dog was off.

'Lovely start to the day,' said Danilo.

'I don't like dogs sniffing at me,' muttered Dad.

From the brim of the slope they could see the whole stinking stretch of the rubbish dump. One way it reached down to the high walls of Hildebrando's timber yard. The other way it climbed up to the grumbling traffic on the highway. There were fires smoking here and there and pigs snuffling at the blackness of the lake in the middle.

'For Christ's sake!' Dad hissed, 'The lorry's here already!'

He was right. The lorry was crawling up the highway between a couple of buses. Ten or twelve people were waiting with forks and sacks up by the track.

'Move it, Danilo!' Dad called.

It was Domingos at the wheel. He drove with one hand dangled out of the window. As he swung the truck in through the gates, Dad waved his sacks.

'OVER HERE! HERE!'

Domingos ignored him. He drove on.

Zivanete was standing with a half-filled sack sagging from her back. She had long, thin arms. She wasn't nearly as old as she looked. The lorry rumbled on and she put a hand up to her headscarf.

'He's heading for the lake!'

'He's not!' shouted Dad, cutting across the rubbish then stepping out on to the track.

'DOMINGOS!' he yelled, 'Dump the rubbish where we can sort it!'

'Clear off!' Domingos shouted. 'I've been told to tip in the lake!'

Others came hurrying down. A short man with a big head of white hair stepped out beside Dad. He was Uncle Macaroni. Macaroni wasn't his real name. And he wasn't anyone's uncle. But that's what everyone called him.

'We won't get anything!' he shouted.

'None of my business!' yelled Domingos, revving the engine so that smoke spat out of the exhaust. But there were five or six people standing in front of the lorry now. Domingos's sunglasses flashed as he looked from one to the next.

'The slope'll collapse if we dump more rubbish up here!'

Dad gritted his teeth. Danilo was coming round the back of the truck. He saw the look on his dad's face. He knew that look.

'Dump the stuff where we can sort it!' Dad yelled. 'Or my boy'll put a fork through your tyres.'

Domingos's face filled the wing mirror. Then the door of the cab swung and the driver jumped down.

'Any part of you that touches my truck, you're not getting back!' he bellowed.

Everyone was looking at Danilo. No one was looking at Dad. And, in an instant, he was up into the cab. He got the lorry in gear and started reversing it up the track. The door was still wide open.

Domingos went off like a firework. He shook his

head. He jabbed the air with his hands. But Dad was gone. The lorry crunched up the track. At the top he tipped the rubbish where everyone could get at it. A cheer went up and the rubbish collectors set off back.

'He's had it!' Domingos hissed.

'He was just trying to help us,' said Danilo.

'What do you know about anything?' snapped Domingos. 'Eh? You're just a piece of black trash.'

'I'm a person same as you,' Danilo told him.

'You're black scum . . . with a clown's haircut,' said Domingos and he aimed a kick at Danilo's leg. 'Brazil would be better off without the lot of you.'

Danilo picked a piece of wood off the ground. Uncle Macaroni put out an arm to hold him back. Domingos paced off towards the lorry.

'Get out of my cab you son-of-a-bitch!' he shouted up.

'Yeah, yeah, yeah,' said Dad, jumping down. 'I didn't damage the truck. I didn't touch you. I've even got an HGV licence. What's the crime?'

'Just shut your mouth and get away from my lorry.'

Domingos pulled himself back into the cab and straightened his sunglasses. Then he called through the window, 'You step out in front of my truck again and I'll run you all down, you ignorant scumbags!'

'You sound like a door squeaking,' said Dad, poking about in the fresh rubbish. That started Uncle Macaroni cackling. Domingos pointed a thick finger out of the window.

'I might do it right now!' he said, revving the engine

and making the lorry jolt forwards. 'Just to wipe those smiles off your ugly black faces!'

'Go and get us some more rubbish,' said Dad.

The gears crunched and Domingos was off.

Danilo and his dad filled eleven sacks that day. Monday was always the best day. Saturday's and Sunday's rubbish came rolled into one. The two of them worked side by side. Dad found the tins and the metal. Danilo found the bottles and the cardboard.

They got four cents a kilo for glass, thirteen cents a kilo for cardboard, fifteen cents a kilo for clear plastic.

'A donkey's pay for a donkey's job,' Dad said. 'But at least there's no goddamn boss.'

When the last of the sacks was tied up, Danilo started trying to get the motor out of a dumped washing machine. The screws came out with a knife and he only had to snap away a part of the casing to pull the motor free.

'Dad!' he called. 'I'm taking this up to Senhor Zuza's.'

'All right,' said Dad, filling the air with a yawn. 'I'll take the sacks to the depot. You do it tomorrow.'

As he came round the side of the shop Danilo whistled, and the bald man leaning on the counter gave him a nod.

'Everything all right, Senhor Zuza?'

'Everything except that hairstyle,' said Senhor Zuza.

Danilo shrugged.

'You think that looks good?' asked the old man.

Danilo shrugged again.

'You look as though you've got a radio stuck to the side of your head.'

'I brought you a washing-machine motor.'

'I can see,' nodded Senhor Zuza. 'Thanks. Stick it over there by the storeroom.'

Danilo put the motor down in the corner. Senhor Zuza filled a cup from the water fountain and handed it to him.

'How's life in the perfumed valley?'

'All right,' nodded Danilo, 'except one of the truck drivers pissing everyone about this morning.'

He launched into the story of what Dad had done. At first Senhor Zuza nodded. Then he laughed. And the more he laughed, the more Danilo remembered details to add to the story: the look on Uncle Macaroni's face, the sound of the truck revving up the hill, the things Domingos had shouted.

'Black scumbags!' Danilo said. 'You believe he called us that?'

'Yes,' nodded Senhor Zuza.

'He's a son-of-a-bitch.'

'There are worse than him,' Senhor Zuza smiled. 'Plenty of people think like him. But they don't all shout it out. It's just a story that nobody cares about the colour of your skin in Brazil. You know . . . we all mix and play samba and football and smile. Sometimes we do. But really it's just a story, Danilo. You know Brazil was just about the last country in the world to free its slaves. And look around . . . it's still the white people who've got the land, the education, the security. We black people live with poverty, with danger. With ignorance. That's the worst of all. The ignorance.'

'Domingos called us ignorant,' said Danilo.

'And we are!' laughed Senhor Zuza. 'You've missed out on school just like I did. You and I are ignorant. Completely ignorant. But it doesn't mean we're stupid. And it doesn't mean we shouldn't try.'

Danilo poured himself some more water and Senhor Zuza carried on.

'It's fifty years since I was your age,' he said. 'And I'll tell you, hardly anything's changed round here. Black people still live at the bottom of the pile. I had one piece of luck. Someone told me to try. And thank God, that's what I did. I tried to lay bricks. I learned to lay bricks. I tried to work with wood. I learned to work with wood. I tried to understand electrics. I learned to be an electrician. And when people didn't trust a black electrician was going to do a good job, I just made *damn sure* that I did. That's how I got this shop. That's how I bought a house for my grandchildren. And that isn't bad for a man who was born with nothing and who was told he'd have nothing in the end.'

Danilo nodded. Then he said, 'Shame you lost all your hair in the process.'

Senhor Zuza picked up a length of hosepipe and swung it at him. Danilo let out a giggle and darted to one side.

'What I'm saying is important, Danilo. *You're* going to have to try. You're good with your hands. You shouldn't be poking around on that dump with the vultures.'

Danilo shrugged. Senhor Zuza tutted.

'What's this shrugging? You know what I've told you. You build yourself a decent handcart and there's a job for you here as a delivery boy.'

A part of Danilo wanted to tell Senhor Zuza that he'd already started getting the things to make a hand-cart. But a part of him knew he'd never really make it. There was silence. He stared at the building materials piled from floor to ceiling. Tools, plugs, fuses, ropes, wheelbarrows, sacks of sand. Then he drank down his water and said, 'Dad'll go mad if I leave him.'

'You sure about that?' asked Senhor Zuza.

Danilo shrugged again. 'I'd still like to work here,' he said.

A customer came in. His neck was glistening with sweat. He shook Senhor Zuza by the hand and Danilo said, 'I'm going to head back.'

'Thanks for the motor,' said the old man.

'Hope it works,' nodded Danilo. 'The last one I brought did, didn't it?'

'No, it didn't,' said Senhor Zuza. 'It was about as good as a pocket in a pair of underpants!'

The customer laughed.

'At least I'm *trying*,' said Danilo.

'Cheerio,' grinned Senhor Zuza.

And Danilo walked back out into the sunlight.

Dad and the others were sitting in the shade down from the tap. Danilo splashed his head with water then wandered across to join them. They were arguing about the way the best Brazilian footballers were all playing for foreign clubs. Nearly everyone was saying it was bad for Brazilian football. Only Uncle Macaroni stayed quiet. And only Dad seemed to think the players were doing the right thing. The argument got louder and louder.

'Hey!' shouted Danilo. 'Let's see what Uncle Macaroni thinks.'

Uncle Macaroni just held out his hands and raised his eyebrows.

'Uncle Macaroni: a man of few words,' sniggered Dad.

'The trouble is I keep on repeating them,' said Uncle Macaroni.

There was a burst of laughter, then quiet.

'Hildebrando's doing some painting,' said Zivanete.

They all looked down the hill. There were two men on scaffolding, painting the walls of the timber yard bright green.

'He's full of money these days,' Dad said. '*Twelve* lorries. I've counted them coming in.'

'Might have chosen a better colour,' said Danilo.

Dad turned down his mouth.

'Makes the building look like a frog with a skin disease.'

Another laugh filled the hot air. Dad looked round at Danilo.

'Senhor Zuza all right then?' he asked.

Danilo nodded.

'How about you?' added Dad.

'I'm all right,' said Danilo.

Dad put an arm round him.

'You're the one thing I've got left,' he said.

As he spoke, a stranger appeared up the track. He was carrying a couple of sacks; a short, stocky man, with narrow eyes.

'There's a Japanese guy coming to join us,' nodded Danilo.

'That's all we need,' said Dad, turning round. Then he smiled. 'That's not a Japanese! It's a bloody Indian.'

They watched the man as he came closer, but the Indian didn't look at them. He had a big, squarish sort of head and long, straight hair.

'Is it like an Indian from the rainforest?' Danilo asked.

'Probably,' said Dad.

Danilo stared.

'I've never seen one of them for real.'

'Where's his bow and arrow?' asked Zivanete.

'They're meant to go about naked, with feathers on their heads,' said Dad. 'This one's got jeans on.'

'And a watch,' nodded Danilo.

'Say something to him,' said Zivanete, nudging Dad with her elbow. Dad brushed at the flies buzzing around.

'He won't even know how to talk the same language as us. They speak some funny red-skin language that goes *chucky nucky hock tock yam yam*.'

He grinned at the Indian. But the Indian walked on without looking round.

The old Kankarurú people told me to protect the earth, the moon, the stars, the thunder. When I look round the white man's city I say, 'It won't work. They have forgotten how to protect these things.'

But I think I have found the place I have come to find. I walk over the lake of rubbish. It stinks bad. But I won't be noticed. There are others – mad people all day carrying sacks, scraping as if they are planting or harvesting. I am carrying sacks, so I seem to be one of them.

In places the ground under my feet breathes the smell of bad dreams. In other places it smells dead. Dead meat. Dead plastic. Dead vegetables. Dead paper. Dead glass.

There are people sitting in the shadow. They are laughing now. There is a boy so black he looks burnt in a fire. And his father, the same. I can hear 'Indian this . . .' and 'Indian that . . .' This is what I get whenever I go beyond our land. Silly questions, jokes. Always with frightened eyes.

OK. I am thinking: call me names. I have work to do for my people. I will take your names. I will eat your names. And I will shit your names.

I cross the rubbish. I have my mission. I will do it, even if I die. I see pigs below. I see a dog passing. A good strong dog. The black father picks up metal, throws it and hits the strong dog.

Then I turn to him. I shout, 'EH! ARE YOU A MAN?'

I raise my hand.

Everyone stared up at the Indian.

'Who's he yelling at?' asked Dad.

'You,' grinned Danilo. 'He didn't like you throwing the tin at the dog.'

'Well, he can get stuffed,' said Dad. 'Look at him. Standing there like Moses on the mountain.'

Uncle Macaroni gave a cackle. Dad called up, 'If you

want to hang around, you can help us fill some sacks with bottles. If not, you can stick a bone in your nose and shut up.'

The stranger stared. The look on his face didn't change.

Then he said, 'You are like a monkey!'

Dad furrowed his brow.

'What was that?' he shouted back.

'Hurting dogs is not for a man,' said the Indian. 'Hurting dogs is for a monkey.'

Dad was up on his feet straight away.

'If I want your opinion I'll give it to you, lad! Now shut your mouth before I tie knots in your ears and send you back to your red-skin friends!'

The Indian raised his hand again.

'My people are not called *red skin*,' he said. 'They are called *Kankarurú*.'

At that a great bawl of laughter broke out around Danilo.

'He's from the kangaroo tribe!' cackled Uncle Macaroni. 'They paint their faces and jump up and down all day.'

He and Dad started jumping about making pow-wow noises. Zivanete bared her teeth and rocked with laughter. Danilo smiled. But once they'd danced round two or three times he'd had enough of the joke.

The air was hot and still. Up by the tap, a vulture was poking at a fish. It had pushed its head right inside, so that the fish's mouth opened and closed. Danilo didn't feel like sitting around any more. He got up. He wondered if he might find that pair of wheels.

He headed towards the egg-lorry slope. The egg lorry came from a chicken farm. What it dumped stank so bad that hardly anyone ever went up that way. It meant Danilo sometimes found good stuff there. He trudged his way up, round the shell of an old car, and suddenly found himself face-to-face with the Indian. Close-up he looked bigger. He was crouched in the shade. Danilo saw something shiny hanging inside his shirt. He thought the Indian was going to speak, but he didn't.

'You all right?' Danilo asked.

The Indian nodded. Then he looked away. He stared off into the distance as though Danilo wasn't worth talking to.

Danilo stood there.

'That lot were only playing about,' he said.

The Indian didn't reply. Danilo tried again.

'You'd like them if you got to know them.'

'Why should I trust white-skin people? Why should I trust black-skin people?' asked the Indian. 'I trust my people. I am here for my people. Understand?'

Danilo shrugged.

'If you want to make some money I can show you the best stuff to collect.'

The Indian turned down his mouth.

'Keep your help,' he said.

He didn't speak again. And Danilo didn't want to stand about like a fool. So he walked on. He looked up the slope. There was nothing but broken eggs and chicken dung. He looked down. There were all sorts of things dumped in a dip in the slope: a fridge, a mattress and a trolley, upside down, with its wheels sticking up in the air.

The black boy has honest eyes. But I am not here to talk to him. He goes away. I get up. I am going to cross the rubbish, away from the people. I walk sideways. It is steep. The sky is hot. The smell is sweet, sour, sweet, sour.

Then my feet drop. The land drops. Everything drops on my head.

Danilo had seen the dump slip before. There was never time to react. There was a *SWISH*, then the rubbish came thudding, flopping down. His first thought was that he'd lost a good pair of wheels. The rubbish pounded on to the trolley, tipping it up then burying it under. But, at the same instant, there was a shout from behind him. It was the Indian. The whole of the slope where he'd been sitting had slipped. And he'd gone with it.

Dad and the others were staring up at the dust.

'THE INDIAN'S CAUGHT IT!' Danilo shouted.

And they all got straight to their feet. Everyone had been buried or partly buried before. The difference was that the Indian was underneath what the egg lorry dumped. And he was right under.

'Use your hands, not your forks,' hissed Dad. 'We don't know where his head is.'

'Easy!' called Zivanete scrambling up the slope. 'Looks as if more of it could come down!'

'But we've got to be quick!' shouted Danilo. 'The guy can't breathe!'

They pulled away armfuls of dirt and feathers and it was Danilo who spotted the light-brown toes.

'HERE!' he yelled.

'He's upside down!' called Uncle Macaroni.

'Typical bloody Indian,' muttered Dad. 'The son-of-a-bitch even has to get buried different to everyone else.'

They managed to get one thick calf free. Then the other leg appeared bent double. Dad shook it, but it just flopped in his hand.

'We've got to pull him now!' Dad shouted. 'He's been under too long!'

So they did. Three people grabbed each leg and they strained upwards. Out he came. Slowly. Stomach. Chest. Neck. Then his head.

And he was smiling. His hair, his face, his whole body were grey with dust and feathers. But he had such a big smile on his face it looked as if he had two people's teeth in his mouth.

Zivanete put her hands round his cheeks.

'You all right?' she asked.

The Indian breathed for a few moments. Then he spat dirt and feathers from his mouth.

'Now I can die!' he said. 'I've been to the bottom of the world and come out the other side. Now I am ready.'

Danilo and the others stood and stared. The Indian got to his feet. Then he put a hand on Zivanete's chest.

'Thank you. Good heart,' he said.

He did the same to each of them.

'Thank you. Good heart.'

Uncle Macaroni bowed solemnly when it was his turn. Dad nodded. Danilo was last. He tried not to smile, but he couldn't help it.

'Danilo! Show him the tap so that he can have a wash,' said Dad.

As Danilo led the Indian down the slope, Dad sniffed, 'Didn't seem such a bad lad.'

'It might have been any one of us half dead in that chicken shit,' shrugged Zivanete.

'Might have been Danilo,' said Dad.

Zivanete nodded.

'This is no place for a boy his age,' tutted Dad.

Zivanete nodded again. 'He's smart enough to end up somewhere better,' she said.

'I'd love him to,' said Dad. 'I'd love him to find a way to get the hell out of here.'

The black boy takes me to the water tap. He says his name is Danilo. I say my people call me Tatatin. It means 'Smoke'.

I say he should leave this place and find another way to live. I say the Great Father is ashamed of a young man creeping about in rubbish. He says maybe.

The black boy Danilo asks where I am from. I say from my people's reserve far away. The reserve is ninety hectares.

He asks if I can kill animals with a bow and arrow. I say we use rifles. I know how to use a rifle fine. He asks if we eat monkeys. I say yes and we also eat honey.

He wants to know what I wear round my neck. My necklace.

'Is it gold?' he asks.

'Gold,' I say. 'From the river near our village. Found by my father's mother.'

'Is there still gold in the river?'

'Little,' I tell him.

We come to the tap. I wash. It is better. The black boy Danilo looks at my watch. He says it is a Japanese watch. He says I am not an Indian because I have a Japanese watch. It makes me laugh. I say, 'If a Japanese buys a hammock from an Indian, does he stop being a Japanese?'

I laugh and he laughs now. I tell him we have a generator in our village and satellite TV. I always watch football. I tell him I have a camera too. He doesn't believe me. I finish washing, then I show him the camera from my pocket. He asks why I have the camera. I decide to tell him my story. I sit in the low sunlight and say this:

'I am here because white woodcutters are invading our reserve to cut trees. They are cutting big trees. When my relative tried to stop them, they shot him. The white woodcutters think Kankarurú people are nothing. They think they can kill Kankarurú people. They think they can shoot us like forest animals. We want our relatives to be alive. We want our forest. We don't want to lose our way. But we don't want to make war. We want to use the justice system.'

I tell the boy, 'I have found who is sending the white woodcutters: a man called Hildebrando. I have been to the police and to politicians and they say that if I can give the proof they will stop Hildebrando. So I went to a shop and bought the camera. I took photographs of Hildebrando's lorry on our land.'

I show this boy the photographs from my pocket. The white woodcutters. Tree trunks in the lorry. The number plate at the *back: BIP 2222. And I tell the boy that this lorry is coming to Hildebrando's place. I say, 'When it comes, I will take photographs. Then I will have proof. That is my mission.'*

He says he hopes I am lucky. I ask him if his children will live in a better world than us. He says he does not know. I tell him we must think about that. It is getting dark. He says he is going home. I say goodbye to the black boy Danilo, and he says goodbye to me.

Danilo woke early on Tuesday. He felt like getting out before Dad started his coughing and complaining. It was cool and quiet outside. He wondered about going down to the bridge. But he couldn't be bothered. It had been like that for weeks. He had the wood and the tools he needed, but he couldn't get started. He decided he'd look for another motor or a TV tube to take up to Senhor Zuza.

He climbed the slope and crossed the track. No one was about. Just some vultures coughing at each other up ahead. It looked like there'd been another slip in the night. He had to scramble up a fresh mound of rubbish. The vultures hopped sideways as he came near. Then he stopped. There was a man slumped on the other side, with a dog sniffing at his back.

'Hey!' Danilo called down.

The dog looked up. But the man didn't move.

Some of the rubbish collectors drank themselves stupid. Danilo had seen them sleeping sprawled out like that. But this guy looked worse than usual. His head was twisted down into the rubbish.

'Hey!' Danilo called again, jogging down the mound.

The dog backed off. Then Danilo realized who it was.

'Tatatin?' he said.

The Indian didn't move. Danilo tugged his arm. Tatatin's head lolled over to the side. Danilo knew he was dead. His mouth sagged open. Both eyes were half shut. His cheeks were swollen and caked with blood. One lip was torn. Danilo turned and ran.

It was early but it was already hot as Domingos's lorry came crawling along the highway. His arm hung casually out of the window but his face looked tense. He expected to see the usual clutch of rubbish collectors waiting as he swung in through the gate. But no one was about. He carried on down the track. Then he spotted them. They were standing off to the left, all of them looking down at the ground.

Danilo heard the truck rumble by. But he didn't look round.

'Poor lad,' said Zivanete.

'Someone beat him inside out,' said Danilo.

Uncle Macaroni shook his head. And Dad breathed out noisily.

'The best we can do is get the body to the police station up the highway.'

Danilo and the others went off to find a hammock and wood to make a stretcher. Dad stayed standing over the body. After a time he reached down and tried to straighten it out. He tugged Tatatin round by one of his shoulders. As he did, the Indian's shirt fell open and out tumbled the gold nugget.

There was a hiss from down by the lake. The back of Domingos's lorry slowly tilted and the rubbish spilled into the water. Domingos reversed.

'The scumbags can stop me now, if they want,' he muttered.

Then he turned the lorry back towards the gate.

Coming up the track he could see Danilo's dad standing on his own. And now he knew what they'd all been staring at: a body stretched out on the rubbish.

The first thing Dad thought was that gold was no use to the Indian. The second thing he thought was that if he didn't take it some policeman would. The third thing he thought was that with some money in his pocket Danilo could get off the dump. He reached down and snapped the string.

Domingos saw him do it. He radioed for the police as he got to the gate on to the highway. He told them what he had seen. Then he clipped the radio on to the dashboard and said, 'If the black bastard gets it in the neck it serves him damn well right.'

Danilo and his dad were still tying together the makeshift stretcher when the police cars came bumping towards them. If Dad had stayed calm things might have worked out differently, but he didn't. He swore at the policemen. He kicked one of them, tried to punch another. Zivanete did her best to calm him down. But one of the policemen grabbed her round the neck. Danilo told them they'd got it wrong. He told them about Hildebrando, Tatatin's camera, the photos of the lorry.

A policeman went through Tatatin's pockets. There

was no camera. There were no photos. Then he went through Dad's pockets and pulled out the gold nugget. They checked Dad's records and found the story about the stolen lorry. Danilo saw the colour drain out of his dad's lips. He noticed the sour smell of his armpits as they pulled him into handcuffs. He was amazed by his dad's sudden silence. Everyone's silence.

'Arrest Hildebrando!' he blurted out. 'My dad's not a murderer! Believe me!'

But blaming a dead Indian on a black nobody seemed to suit the police. Hildebrando owned land. Hildebrando was white. Hildebrando knew the Mayor. Arresting Hildebrando was going to make trouble.

'I saw the photographs!' Danilo yelled as they pushed Dad into a car. 'You've got the wrong man!'

'Prove it!' said the police sergeant. 'Bring us the proof!'

Then the cars were gone. Dad was gone. Zivanete held her hands to her cheeks. Uncle Macaroni was shrugging. And Danilo was walking off across the dump on his own. The saws hadn't started down at the timber yard. There was no one there yet. He was going to find the proof.

Climbing the scaffolding was easy and, from the top, he could see over the roof. Hildebrando's lorries were parked to one side of the yard. All of them were empty except one which was piled high with tree trunks. Danilo recognized the figures on the number plate – BIP 2222.

He shinned on to the roof and crept across the tiles.

There was a fire escape down the far wall. Danilo swung on to it. It was a long way down. Step by step he dropped down into the yard. But a couple of rungs off the bottom there was an explosion of barking. Two Alsatians flew out from under a lorry. Danilo only just yanked himself up quickly enough and, at the same moment, a door opened. Out came a man with a pistol in his belt.

'EH!' he shouted. 'Down here!'

The dogs were going mad, twisting from side to side. Danilo didn't think twice. He scrambled back up the way he'd come, hoisting himself on to the roof again. There was no gunshot, but he heard feet on the ladder. He belted across the roof tiles. But the man was quick. He was up the ladder before Danilo had got to the far side. Ahead were the metal bars of the scaffolding. Danilo had to duck to get through them and, as he did, he glimpsed the guard behind him with the gun in his hand.

He panicked. He threw himself over the bars. The guard shouted, 'Stop! You'll get a bullet!'

Danilo's ankle hit a tin of paint. The tin tipped up. He was thrown off balance. Next thing, he, the tin and a gallon of green paint were falling through the air.

The wall flashed by. Paint splattered across Danilo's face. Then he hit the ground with the biggest thud he'd ever felt. But he was on something soft. It was a pile of rubbish bags in a sort of enclosure out the back of the yard.

'EH!' came the man's voice, from somewhere above.

Everything was covered in green paint. Danilo

scrambled up to his feet. One foot skidded from under him. The fence round the rubbish wasn't high. So he leaped at it, scrabbled over and dropped down the other side.

He could still hear the click of the guard's feet on the roof tiles, but the guard could not see him now. And he knew where he was. He was at the top of the slope that led to the bridge. He darted for the undergrowth and, moments later, was down to the opening under the bridge.

Once inside he stayed put. Hours passed. He imagined Hildebrando's guards kicking him in the head, beating him numb. He imagined Dad's voice booming out at the police station. He imagined what he'd do if Dad got locked up. He had paint down his neck and his arms. He was hungry, thirsty. But he sat there. Nothing seemed to move.

It was the hammer that did it. He'd been staring at the wood and the nails without really seeing them. Then he looked at the hammer where he'd dropped it the day before and he decided: 'I'm going to find some wheels. I'm going to make this thing.'

He got up. He dropped into the stream and washed the paint off best as he could. Then he climbed, through the undergrowth, back to the dump.

The sun was hot. But Danilo didn't care about the sun. He walked the dump from end to end. Sweat streamed down his neck, his back. He saw a smashed stereo. He saw a headless doll. He saw newspapers. He saw tyres. He saw an album of someone's wedding photographs. He saw pigs. He saw bruised fruit. He shook his head to keep the flies off his face. But no wheels.

When he was too tired to walk any more, he sat in the shade by the gate. The nerves in his legs were trembling. One of the afternoon lorries clunked past. He watched it with a hollow look in his eyes. Uncle Macaroni and a couple of others pitched up with their forks.

Danilo watched the back of the lorry tilt. The rubbish tumbled out like a wave on a beach. He saw Uncle Macaroni hacking about in the puffed-up black bags. Then something caught his eye. He got to his feet. Five or six of the rubbish bags were splashed with green paint.

Uncle Macaroni and Zivanete helped. They went through everything in those bags. They found Tatatin's camera, smashed open. They found torn photographs of Hildebrando's lorry on the Indians' land. It was proof. The police couldn't argue. They let Dad go.

Early on Thursday, Dad was back, waiting with the others as the first lorry arrived. Danilo had wandered off on his own.

'Danilo! For Christ's sake!' Dad shouted. 'The lorry's here!'

Danilo didn't turn round. He was off across the rubbish, looking about for something.

'Leave him be,' shrugged Zivanete. 'He doesn't deserve to be shouted at. Not just when he's shown us the good sense he's got in his head.'

'And God knows where he got that from,' said Uncle Macaroni. 'Not from his father.'

Dad scratched his chin and laughed.

'Aren't many lads round here with a head like his,' he said.

'Not since I gave him that haircut,' said Zivanete.

Uncle Macaroni let out a cackle. The lorry pulled up. As they walked towards it, Dad peered over his shoulder again.

'He acts like there's something worth finding up there.'

'Some chance,' said Uncle Macaroni.

Sean Taylor went to school in Wimbledon and to university in Cambridge. He now spends part of his life in England and part of it in Brazil, where his wife is from. To write 'Smoke' he spent time with families who work on a rubbish dump at the edge of a town in Brazil. He would like to send thanks to Senhor Benedito Tomé, who helped make that visit possible.

Assignment Day

by Nick Gifford

A fantasy story

It snowed on Assignment Day, and the heavy fall reduced the world to whites, greys and a few shades of brown where the horses and carts turned it to slush in the road. The colours suited Dean's mood.

Assignment Day. The day when Educational Audit would confirm what everyone already knew: that he and his twin brother Leo were straight Fours, just like their parents, and their parents before them.

Assignment Day. The last day of the year in which you passed your thirteenth birthday. The day when your future was assigned to you, based entirely on what Ed. Audit called your 'predispositions'. You are, as the official guidelines said, what you were born.

Assignment Day was a formality, really: you always follow your parents, your family, your racial group, whether you want to or not.

'Hey, Dean!'

He looked up from the rutted slush on the pavement,

just in time to duck a spray of snow aimed at his head.

'Not like that – like this!' He scooped some snow from the wall, squeezed it into a ball and hurled it at Jena. She was a small target, even though she was wrapped up in a big, fur-lined coat that reached her ankles. Her skin was almost as pale as the new snow, a clear sign of her high status.

She had ducked even before he released the snowball. 'Saw it coming. You'll have to be quicker than that, Four-boy.'

From anyone else, the name would have stung, but Dean knew that Jena was just trying to wind him up. He raised his hands in surrender. 'What's the point?' he said, laughing and allowing her to shower him with snow from another badly-formed snowball. 'You'll just Sight it again.'

Jena was going to be Un-numbered. Like her parents, her family, her race. The Un-numbered had various Talents, both magical and otherwise. In Jena's case that Talent was the Sight: untrained as yet, her gift meant that she could peer just a little way into the future. It didn't work all the time, but it was certainly good for dodging snowballs. By the time she graduated from school her Talent would be far more refined and she would end up with some high-powered Council forecasting job.

The Un-numbered ruled the world. It was the natural role for their kind, of course.

'Scrap! Scrap! Scrap!'

There was a group ahead, gathered around two fighting boys. Dean didn't need the gift of Sight to

136

know that one of them would be his brother, Leo.

He rushed forwards and pushed his way through the group. Leo was on the ground, and a big, golden-haired boy – Rufus! of course it would be Rufus – held him by the hair at the back of his head and was rubbing his face in the slush.

'Make the snow stick,' Rufus was saying. 'Let's make your face as pale as the rest of us, dark-boy.'

Dean stepped forwards. In truth, Leo's skin wasn't much darker than the others', but that wasn't the point. He was going to be a Four, like Dean, and they all knew it.

Dean met Rufus's look.

'Let him go, Rufus,' he said. 'You've won.' And he always would. Rufus was destined to be Un-numbered, just like Jena, only his Talent was psychokinetic. He could control other objects, including people, with the power of his mind. That was why Leo's body was pinned down in the mud while Rufus only appeared to be holding his head.

Rufus glared at Dean and for a moment it seemed that he would turn his attention on the younger of the twins. Then he shrugged, and ran a hand through his shaggy hair. 'Fair do,' he said. 'Leo needs to learn his place, or he'll get far more than a face full of horse dung and snow. The trouble with your kind is you think you're just as good as the rest of us.'

With that, he laughed and went off to join his friends in the watching group.

Dean and Jena went to help Leo to his feet, but they were shrugged off.

'No need to thank me,' said Dean. 'No need at all.'

Leo stood and rubbed at his face, then spat into the road. 'He called me a Twelve-lover,' he said. Twelves were the lowest of them all: dark-skinned, uneducated, living on welfare or out working the fields and cleaning the streets. 'He called me a Four . . . a dark-boy.'

Leo's skin, normally a shade or two darker than Jena's, now burned an angry red. His dark eyes darted about restlessly, as if he were looking for Rufus, ready to pick another fight. Leo never knew when it was better to let things rest.

It was funny, Dean thought. For thirteen years they had all mixed pretty much as equals. There were differences and arguments, of course. It was always fairly obvious if you came from one of the pale-skinned Unnumbered families, or from the darker Twos and Fours, or whatever (the school didn't accept anyone lower than a Five) – but the divisions hadn't been important. Yet as Assignment Day had approached the differences came to matter more and more, so that fights and name-calling had become commonplace.

'And . . .?' said Jena. 'Leo, dear, allow me to let you in on a little secret. You *are* a Four. Or you will be after today.'

Educational Audit was based in one of the Council buildings near the centre of town. It was a tall, grey block with narrow windows and steam billowing from chimneys high on its sloping roof. One of the teachers Dean barely knew had them line up two by two before a small door and slowly they shuffled forwards until they were inside.

Dean queued with Jena, with Leo a couple of places ahead of them.

'Not one little bit,' said Jena into the silence.

'Will you miss this place when you go away to school?' Dean asked a split second later and then laughed. She definitely had a gift for foresight.

'I'll miss the people, though,' she added.

'You'll make new friends.'

'I don't want new friends. Still, there are the holidays, I suppose.'

Dean's parents had done well to get him and Leo into one of the best schools in the city, to be taught with the children of the Un-numbered and the best of the One-to-Fives. But after Assignment Day all that would change. The Un-numbered would go away to their academy and all the others would start to train for the futures set out for them in their bloodlines.

Leo had always claimed that this system was unfair, but how else could it be? This was how the world worked. It could be a lot worse than growing up a Four, Dean thought.

He and Jena reached a desk where a man sat peering at a thick book full of names. He was a small man with pale brown skin like Dean's. He had a shiny, bald head, a neat little moustache and thick spectacles. Tattooed in the centre of his forehead was the number '4.128' – a label that described exactly who he was and how he would live.

Dean saw his own future behind that desk: a junior

clerical role in the Council, or one of the institutes, a job that would make good use of his natural eye for detail and order. It was a role he had been born to. He wondered why it was that he didn't feel more enthusiastic about this, if it really was his destiny.

The clerk checked their names off on his list and waved them through another doorway into a large waiting room.

They waited as, one by one, their fellow thirteen-year-olds were called for and led away into the depths of the Ed. Audit building, later to re-emerge with their futures sealed.

Dean first suspected that something was wrong when Leo didn't come back out after his test, even though others who had entered after him were coming out.

He stood and walked around, trying to peer through the door whenever it opened to see if he could work out what was happening.

Coming back to his seat he caught sight of Jena's face. She was struggling to suppress her excitement.

'What is it?' he asked. 'Why is Leo taking so long?'

'I don't know,' she said, frustratingly. 'I can't tell. But as soon as he went through I knew that *something* was going to happen. Maybe he's been mis-assigned!'

'Yeah,' said Rufus, from nearby. 'He's a straight Twelve. I knew he belonged out in the fields with the wogs.'

But Dean was barely listening. *Mis-assigned*. It was possible. That was why Ed. Audit held this exercise,

140

after all: tests to confirm everyone's status. Tests to spot any earlier mistakes . . .

He heard his name called.

He looked at Jena and she was grinning. 'Go for it,' she told him. 'Just . . . go for it!'

The examiner could easily have been the clerk who had checked everyone in on the big register, although at a second glance Dean saw that he was older, with grey flecks in his moustache and fringe of hair.

'Name?'

'Dean Everian.'

'Anticipated assignment?'

'I . . . I don't know.' Not any more.

The examiner paused and looked at him oddly. 'We have you down as an anticipated 4.064 to 4.180 here.'

Dean shrugged.

'Your Pre-assignment Tests from school concur with expectations: they indicate that you are of a racial sub-type that is well suited to detailed work. Your parents work in the Administration, don't they?'

Dean ignored the question. 'What happened to my brother?' he said. 'Leo Everian. He came in before me.'

'I am not at liberty to discuss individual cases,' said the examiner. 'It is important that we follow procedure. You should know that such things matter to a Four. Good administration runs on an adherence to procedures, don't you know.'

The examiner was on edge, Dean realized. The sweat glistening on his brow was not a result of the room's warmth, it came from nervous tension. The dartings of his eyes from side to side confirmed his state. The examiner was hiding behind his procedures.

What was going on?

'A small blood test,' said the examiner, gesturing at a box-like contraption on the desk between them. 'Please insert your left hand.'

There was a hole facing Dean. He put his hand inside and felt his forefinger gripped in a cold ring of metal. He flinched at a sudden pinprick, more in surprise than pain. When he withdrew his hand he saw a small red spot where the needle had sampled his blood.

The examiner typed something in, using the keypad on the other side of the box. 'The results will come through in a few minutes,' he said. He gestured to a door on the far side of the room, and continued, 'You will take a written test now. Please go through. You will find all that you need in the next room.'

Dean went through, and shut the door softly behind him. Before him there was a chair and a desk, with some sheets of paper and a pencil. He sat, turned the paper over and tried to concentrate on the questions. If he was a good Four then this should be no problem: a task to be completed.

The questions seemed to be fairly standard intelligence tests: mathematics, reasoning, puzzle-solving. But some of the puzzles were not soluble by normal means. 'The walls of the next room are painted a certain colour. What colour are they?' Jena would get that one right! 'How long have you been given for this test?' He realized that the examiner had not told him.

They were testing for special Talents alongside the more ordinary questions.

The walls in this room were dove-grey, as they had been in every room in the building, so he supposed that they would be the same in the next room. He did not know what that answer would tell them about him, other than that he took the safe option – another Four trait, he thought. He had no idea how long they would have for the questions. As long as he needed, he hoped. He wrote that down, and continued with the test.

As he completed the final question, the far door opened and a woman with '4.820' tattooed across her brow beckoned him through.

He waited in a chair in a corridor with cream walls, as administrators and examiners hurried in both directions, clutching files and books and stacks of paper.

A door opened and a man in grey nodded towards him. 'Master Everian,' he said. 'Please come through.'

No one had ever called him that before.

'Please sit, Master Everian,' said the man, gesturing at a plush leather chair.

He sat opposite Dean, clutching a file defensively on his lap. He was a tall, pale-skinned man and in the centre of his forehead was the number '2.122'. A senior examiner, then.

'It appears . . . it seems that there has been an administrative irregularity, Master Everian. A mis-interpretation of status re racial categorization and sub-grouping.'

Dean looked at him, and wished he would talk in a language he understood.

'You have been mis-assigned,' said the man.

'How? What does that mean?'

'Your Pre-assignment Test was 4.071, but that is quite clearly wrong.'

Dean thought of Rufus's jibe. 'I'm a Twelve, aren't I?' he said softly. The lowest of the low.

At this the man smiled. 'No, Master Everian. No you most certainly are not. You are without Assignment.'

Dean stared at him. Un-numbered. Like Jena and the foul Rufus! He rubbed at one cheek with his fingers, as if the colour might come off. 'But what about this? I am not pale like Jena and the others.'

'But you are not as dark as most Fours,' said the man. That was true, Dean acknowledged. 'There is a paleness in you, Master Everian, and Talent, too. The blood tests do not lie.'

'What about my brother?'

The man dipped his head. 'We are not at liberty to discuss individual cases,' he said. But it was clear that Leo, too, had been re-assigned. *Un*-assigned.

'I must have a Talent,' he said, his brain racing, thinking aloud.

The man nodded. 'Gifts tend to emerge in adolescence,' he told Dean. 'Some later than others. You may still be unaware of your particular Talent. It may be something that you take for granted, or it may be something that has not yet emerged clearly enough for you to recognize it for the gift that it is.'

Dean thought hard, but it was no good. He had no special Talent.

The man raised the file he had been clutching.

'Looking through your records, you appear to have the knack of getting your own way. There is a Talent, one of the less common gifts, that allows its holder to influence others. The power of persuasion. It is a very valuable Talent to have.'

Immediately, Dean pictured Rufus holding Leo down in the snow. Dean had told him to release his twin and Rufus had done so. He thought then of that question in the exam: *How long have you been given for this test?* His answer had been that he hoped they would give him as long as he needed and, sure enough, that lady had come into the room just as he completed the last question. He wondered how long she had waited outside. Had he held her there against her will, waiting until he had finished?

He couldn't believe it.

But then . . . he couldn't disbelieve it, either.

'Our parents . . .' he said. 'They knew, didn't they?'

The man nodded. 'It's part of your inheritance,' he said. 'The people who raised you are probably not your true parents. You would have been adopted, or at the least your real father must be another man . . .'

Suddenly, he felt himself about to burst with anger – at the way this man so calmly discussed his family, at the secrets and lies that had led up to this point, at *everything*. He realized now that he had always been treated according to his expected future: the teachers at school had always favoured the Un-numbered. He had always been a lowly Four in everyone's eyes. They had all judged him by his origins and his race – even his friends, even Jena.

That was when he made his decision.

He looked at the examiner, and waited until the man would meet his eyes. He smiled and the man smiled nervously in return.

It was time to put his powers of persuasion to the test.

He found Leo and Jena playing in the yard outside the Ed. Audit building, kicking about in the snow and squealing like little children.

Jena spotted him first and she ran across and hugged him, then Leo joined them and they hugged and danced around in the snow.

'I knew it!' squeaked Jena. 'I just *knew* it! I always thought you guys were a cut above. I just couldn't work out why.'

'Re-assigned,' said Leo, still disbelieving. 'I always knew that we were meant for better things. I always knew that we were destined for more than being stuck for fifty years in a huge office in the depths of the Administration.'

Dean nodded. It was true that he had felt like that, too. 'Sure,' he said. 'But don't you think that *all* the Fours feel that way?' He thought of the examiners and administrators he had seen today: each of them, wrapped up in their own little worlds, but they must all dream. Didn't they *all* resent the boundaries put on their lives from birth?

'Sure,' said Leo, not getting it at all. 'But we've been re-assigned, little brother! Un-numbered! We're part of the elite, the ruling race!'

Jena was studying Dean closely. Suddenly, she wasn't happy. Quietly, she said, 'You've done something stupid, haven't you?'

Leo fell quiet, and the two of them stared at Dean.

He shrugged. 'What's your gift, big brother?'

'I don't know. It hasn't emerged yet. There's plenty of time. What's your point?'

'My Talent is a rare one,' said Dean. 'I have the power of persuasion. I can influence people so much that they just have to go along with what I want.'

'You always did get your own way, you little –'

'What have you done?' interrupted Jena.

'I used my Talent. I persuaded the examiner that there had been a mistake. Why should my fate be decided by which group I'm born into? Why should our bloodlines decide who lives in a palace and who works in the fields? I'm not playing that game, big brother.'

They just stared at him.

Eventually, Jena said, 'So you've thrown it all away . . .'

'You've got it all wrong, little brother,' said Leo. 'Wherever your gift is, it definitely isn't in the brains department.' He shook his head, still not believing Dean's actions. 'It's the natural order, isn't it? The Un-numbered have the Talents. They have to be the ruling race. It's only natural. We all know that. And it's only right that they – that *we* should be rewarded for that.

'And look at the others, will you? The Elevens. They're short and strong and dark – of course they work underground. That's what they're suited for, isn't it? And the Twelves. They're just built for working in the fields for all the hours of the day. They don't have the brains for anything else, but they can keep on labouring for hours after a Four would have flaked out in the sun. It's only natural. Just like they have good rhythm. It's in the breeding. It's . . .'

Leo was running out of steam, shaking his head. Unlike Dean, he did not have the gift of persuasion.

'You sound like Rufus,' said Dean, disappointed.

'So? Maybe he knows what he's talking about.'

Dean turned away from his brother and started to walk. When he looked back, he saw the two of them heading away in the other direction, Leo still talking and Jena nodding, agreeing, trying to calm him.

This was the first time he had seen his father's place of work. It was a wide room, as large as the main hall at school, but with a ceiling so low that Dean could almost touch it if he stretched up. Row upon row of desks were crammed into this vast office, each with identical typing machines, abacuses, pencil-holders, trays and other items Dean couldn't identify. The typing machines were fed with long rolls of paper that appeared to go from one machine to another to another for the entire length of the room and were covered in columns of numbers and strange symbols. The noise of clacking keys and counting beads was extraordinary. No wonder his parents were both hard of hearing.

'How did you get in here . . .?'

'I spoke to your column supervisor,' said Dean. 'I told him it was important. I can be very persuasive.'

'You know, I take it,' said his father.

Dean nodded. 'Leo and I were mis-assigned. There was an administrative irregularity, or whatever the examiner called it.'

'I'm not your real father,' said the man before him. 'Your mother . . . she knew someone else for a short time. One of the Un-numbered. He was very persuasive . . .'

There was a long silence.

'I loved your mother. I still do. We all make mistakes.'

'Me and Leo. We're her mistakes.'

The man shrugged. 'You don't plan these things to happen,' he said. 'I may not be your real father, but I've brought you up as my son and I've loved you as much as anyone ever could. I got you both into the best school I could so that you would be ready if things should turn out like this. I always knew that this day would come and we would lose the two of you.'

'I don't have to go, Father. I could stay. I can do that.'

His father looked at him, puzzled. 'But why would you want to do that? You're not our kind, Dean. You're better. Your kind – you're a race apart, a race *above*. You need to take your opportunity. We'll still see you at holidays, after all. If you want, that is. The choice is yours.'

'But I don't want to be a part of all that,' said Dean. 'I want it to be different.'

His father fixed him with a hard look. 'Good,' he said. 'That's great. So try to change it!' He waved a hand, indicating the wide open office, the hundreds of

149

desks and typing machines and hard-working Fours and Fives labouring away. 'But tell me, Dean: do you think you can change the system working somewhere like this?'

The snow was thawing, and colour was edging back into the world once again.

Everything had happened so quickly! Only a week ago they had been queuing up at the Ed. Audit building to take their turn at the Assignment Day tests and now . . .

Dean sat with Jena on the train. Leo sat across from them.

'I'm really looking forward to it but I'm still nervous, even though I know it's going to work out fine!' she said. 'I knew you wouldn't be such a fool for long, Dean. You could never choose to be a boring Four over this: the chance of a whole new start in the Academy of the Un-numbered.'

The train was rounding a bend, steam from the locomotive blocking the view from the window. When it cleared, Dean saw an open field, rows of green shoots emerging through what remained of the snow. In the distance, a group of Twelves were working away at clearing a ditch, knee-deep in the icy mud and no doubt loving their natural role in the way the world worked.

'It's an opportunity,' Dean agreed.

After seeing his father, he had gone straight back to Ed. Audit and talked his way into seeing the senior examiner who had told him of the 'administrative irregularity'. It had been easy enough to persuade him to check his paperwork again, and spot that Dean should, in fact, be reclassified back to Un-numbered status. The man was most apologetic and started calling him Master Everian again.

His father was right: if he was going to change the system then he might as well start from a position of power.

He looked at Leo and Jena, both so happy with their place in the so-called 'natural order'. Changing attitudes was going to be a tough challenge, but then . . . if anyone could start persuading people it was Dean Everian!

Nick Gifford's first novel, Piggies, *was published in 2003, and his second,* Flesh and Blood, *in 2004. Born in Harwich, Essex, he and his young family recently settled a few miles down the coast in Brightlingsea. You can find out far too much about Nick and his work at www.nickgifford.co.uk.*

Beads

by Manjula Padmanabhan

A story set in modern-day Delhi, India

Jenny bent to see how Farida was getting along with the stitching only to straighten up a moment later, exclaiming. 'Oh – !' she said, 'that's . . . *exquisite!*' She turned around to her sister standing behind her and said, 'Mary – have a look at this!' Then she returned to the girl, who was sitting cross-legged on the floor, saying, 'My dear, you're really very clever – did you know that?'

Farida glanced up to meet the older woman's gaze then down again, very quickly. Pleasure at the praise flushed through her. But she bit her lower lip to prevent herself from smiling. That might be considered unseemly. The most she permitted herself by way of a response was, 'Thank you . . .' in a very low, very respectful voice. The attention embarrassed her and she stirred the tiny container of pale pink beads in her hand with the tip of her needle, not daring to look up.

She had chiselled features, her mouth a perfect Cupid's bow over a softly swelling crescent. Her skin was the colour of unsweetened chocolate. Her only adornments were a silver nose-stud and a trace of shiny black *kajal* outlining the lower lids of her large, expressive eyes. Her hair was oiled and combed back tight from her forehead, with one or two tendrils hanging loose beside her cheeks. A transparent sky-blue headscarf fell in graceful folds down over her shoulders and to her waist. Beneath it she wore a dark blue *kurta* with matching *salwar*-pyjamas.

Mary was bending too now, to examine the unfinished front panel of the blouse Farida was working on. Petite rosettes fashioned out of pink and blue glass beads, each one hardly wider than a mustard seed, had been worked into the white muslin cloth. It was indeed very dainty work. The girl had not needed to stencil a design. She had produced graceful, free-flowing curves punctuated with tiny leaves and blossoms with the assurance of an instinctive artist.

'I do hope Mickey agrees to wear it,' said Jenny, 'after all the work that's gone into it!'

Mary frowned slightly. 'It would've made more sense, surely,' she remarked, 'if you'd checked with her beforehand . . .'

Jenny, still admiring the beadwork, sighed. 'She was in one of her moods. Said she didn't need my suggestions for clothing. Refused to discuss it.' She smiled ruefully as she stood up. 'She's so resentful of me! Been that way ever since the divorce. Everyone says she'll get over it, but she's certainly taking her time.' She shook the blouse out so that she could get an impression of its general size and shape, holding it against her chest. 'I suppose it would even fit me, at a pinch,' she said, 'it's that loose. What d'you say? Too youthful?' She continued without waiting for an answer from her sister. 'It'll be a shame though, if Mickey doesn't want it. It's so pretty . . .' Her voice was wistful.

Even after they had returned the material to Farida, the two English *memsahibs* remained where they were, on the long front veranda of Mary's first-floor flat. The harsh glare of the north Indian summer was kept at bay by fine bamboo *chicks*. Broad-leaved potted plants filled one end of the veranda. At the other end was the door to the guest bedroom in which Jenny and Mickey were staying. Overhead, a ceiling fan agitated the humid air with a busy *clickety-clack-clickety-clack* sound.

Farida sat on a white-and-black cotton *durrie*, beside the plants. Her beads were stored in two sets of round stackable containers. Both stacks were dismantled now, their sections arrayed in front of her like a painter's palette. One stack contained round beads in delicate shades – turquoise blue, moonbeam white, pearl pink, duckweed green. The other stack contained rectangular beads like polished grains of rice, in strong colours: black, red, orange, gold and silver. On a low platform, to one side, was her father's old hand-operated sewing machine. He had been an itinerant tailor for many years, doing the rounds of his regular customers in the stately homes of the capital city. Then a road accident crippled him, keeping him house-bound. Farida was the eldest of his three daughters by his first wife. She was the only one with an aptitude for using the machine. When an offer for work had come to him via the press-*wallah* who serviced the foreigners' house, he sent Farida in his place. The machine would remain in the house for the duration of the work, because it was too heavy for Farida to carry back and forth. It was the first time he had charged her with such a weighty responsibility and she was very conscious of the honour being shown to her in this way.

Farida could understand only disjointed fragments of the conversation of the two pale ladies standing a short distance from her. The visiting *mem* had light yellow hair and seemed younger. The other one, whose house it was, was taller and thinner, with dark brown hair. They both wore short-sleeved white blouses, but the older one wore loose cream-beige slacks while her sister wore a bright pink skirt, gathered at the waist and full at the hem.

Jenny said, several times, an unfamiliar word that sounded a bit like a sneeze: '. . . extraordinary . . .' This was followed by, 'Will she mind doing more?' and, 'I can't imagine such a talent going to waste!'

Mary murmured, 'We can certainly ask her what she thinks . . .'

Then they were both appraising her, apparently, because Jenny said, 'Quite a little beauty, isn't she! Classic features, like the sculptures in the museum yesterday —' This remark filled Farida's head with a sensation so warm and light that she almost ceased to breathe. In all her fifteen years, no one had *ever* said that before! She betrayed no reaction, however. She knew she oughtn't to be listening in on a conversation not intended for her ears.

The two women drifted out of range of Farida's hearing. A moment later, they had stepped through the glass doors of the veranda and into the air-conditioned interior of the flat. A gust of chilly air wafted out to where Farida sat working.

She had just finished one of the front panels of the blouse when another gust of cool air stirred the trailing edge of her headscarf. This time, however, it was from the guest room. Someone had come out from there. Farida glanced up to see who it was, then immediately looked back down again. She guessed it must be Jenny's daughter, Mickey, yet she was confused. The figure had white hair, absolutely short, as if it had been shaved. It was easy to mistake her for a boy except for her clothes. They consisted of little more than a tiny orange top, like a bodice, and a pair of loose black shorts, in some shiny, synthetic material.

The figure came up, slowly, to where Farida sat. Then she knelt down, at the very edge of the *durrie*, staring at Farida's fingers as they worked. Farida bit her lip, feeling self-conscious and uncomfortable, afraid that she would prick her finger out of nervousness and stain the blouse. But she didn't look up or acknowledge the other girl's presence.

A few minutes passed in silence. Then the strange-looking girl-boy bent forwards, in order to catch Farida's attention, and said, 'It's too hot out here. Will you sit inside, please? In my room? I'd like to watch you work.' She spoke slowly and carefully, indicating the guest room.

Farida looked up now, but shrank back. She felt

intimidated even though she realized the other girl was making a friendly offer. She would have liked to say she was perfectly comfortable where she was but wasn't confident enough of her English. So she shook her head mutely, staring at the other girl. At close quarters, she looked alarming. Her eyes were like blue glass marbles but outlined in thick black make-up, so that she looked as if she were wearing a mask. Her lips were painted black too. She had silver rings pierced through the skin of the eyebrows, two on the right side, one on the left. Her skin was translucently pale. Farida could see faint traces of blue veins, near the eyes and at the throat. The sunlight, passing through the slender bamboo strips of the *chicks* behind her, touched her ears with vivid pink lines.

'My name's Michaela – Mickey for short –' said Mickey.

But before she could continue, her aunt Mary had come out on to the veranda. 'Mickey, dear,' she said, 'I'd rather you didn't disturb Farida, please. She's got a lot of work to do and not all that much time in which to get it finished – besides, I think you're making her nervous –'

Mickey looked towards Farida, a mute appeal in her eyes. But Farida knew better than to defy an employer. Keeping her eyes firmly on her embroidery, she returned to work. Sighing, Mickey got to her feet, went back to her room without saying anything to her aunt and slammed the door shut.

It was seven in the evening by the time Farida left for home. She lived in Old Delhi, far to the north of the spacious Sunder Nagar flat in which she'd spent her day. She changed two buses to reach her stop, then another twenty minutes on foot through lanes so narrow that four people could only just walk abreast, with no pavement to speak of. Cyclists, cycle-rickshaws, scooter-rickshaws, hand-cart-*wallahs*, stray dogs and even a couple of gigantic, placid humpbacked bulls competed for passage through those lanes. Every inch of the way was dense with pedestrians, sampling the wares at open-fronted little shops. Each one was barely wider or taller than a lady's dressing table, selling everything from motor spare parts and costume jewellery to audio cassettes and hair ribbons.

The stench of diesel fumes merged with the pungent aroma of onions, chillies and turmeric from countless food stalls to create a potent, suffocating atmosphere. Blindingly bright gas lanterns flared over black cauldrons of boiling oil. Glistening, bare-bodied cooks sat cross-legged on elevated platforms, working like automatons above the fumes. With their right hands they flung savoury batter-dipped *bhujias* or sweet, sticky *jilebis* into the cauldrons, the oil reacting with a furious, spluttering roar. With their left hands, using great flat slotted spoons, they fished out their deep-fried treasures and deposited them in baskets at the front.

Just as quickly as the baskets were filled, they were emptied again by the never-ending tide of hungry customers. Some were returning home from work, some were just starting out on a night shift, some were out for their evening's stroll. From all around, the roaring, hammering, clattering, toot-tooting, parp-parping, rackety-tattering, thunder-throated cacophony formed a continuous backdrop of hard noise.

Farida's father owned three tiny rooms two floors up above street level, deep within the bosom of this area. By the time her feet were on the worn treads of the two iron ladders that led up to her home, night had fallen, though the clamour and the throng continued unabated.

She spent the whole evening telling her two little stepbrothers about the amazing sights and sounds of her day in the Big House. Even her stepmother, Salma-Bi, paused in her preparations for the night meal to listen to Farida's account of her experiences.

By far the most captivating description was that of the young 'Missie-*mem*' whom Farida had not seen till that afternoon, though this was her third day at the house. 'My first thought was, *Who is this boy?* She looked nothing like a girl! Her hair was so short – shorter even than this much –' she said, indicating the nail phalange of her right hand's smallest member, 'and white! White hair! Can you imagine? And yet she was only my own age, perhaps younger! Her skin was transparent! I swear – everything I say is true.'

Eventually, Salma-Bi, growing tired of the attention being diverted in the direction of her stepdaughter, said, 'Oh – enough, enough! It's all very well to fill the children's ears with nonsense! But why not tell us something important for a change? Such as – what did you earn today?' Farida was glad she was able to satisfy Salma-Bi on this account too: 120 rupees for three plain nightshirts and two pairs of *salwars*. Plus there was the blouse that was still being worked on. And . . . she paused before sharing the best news of all: the visiting *mem,* the one who was the mother of the strange-looking girl-boy, had wanted to discuss the possibility of securing Farida's services for a larger commission of work. Maybe as many as two hundred nightgowns and kaftans, she said, all made to order, for some kind of shop or fair. Mary-*mem* said she would have to work it out on paper to see if the project made good financial sense, but her younger sister seemed so excited by the mere prospect of it that Farida supposed it was all but a certainty.

Listening to this, Salma-Bi was mollified enough to grunt her approval, 'Eh! That'll be the first good thing to come of you so far – if it happens! Who can say, how much of what you understood was true? I for one can't understand one single word of that *kitti-pitti-kitti-pitti* sound the foreigners make when they talk –' Then she held out her hand, expecting to be given Farida's wages for the day. Farida handed the money over willingly, knowing that her father would hear a good account of his eldest daughter, for once.

Later, while washing up after everyone had eaten, Farida caught a glimpse of her own face in the shiny surface of the stainless-steel plate in her hands. *Me, beautiful? No! I must have misunderstood what they said!* she thought to herself. All her life, her own mother having died when she was only five years old, she had known only the continuous jibes and jeers of her stepmother. Salma-Bi never let a day pass without reminding her that, 'black as a buffalo' as she was, she would never find a husband, so she had best accustom herself to earning her own living. Salma-Bi was hardly one to talk: she was the colour of a sturdy earthen pot, brown and hardy. But her two sons had taken Farida's father's fair colour and Farida's own younger sisters were also pale skinned. Already, though they were not yet teenagers, there was a murmuring and a shifting amongst the grandmothers of the locality. Already, future suitors were being identified amongst the eligible boys. Already, the girls wore their headscarves with a certain coquettish awareness of how to frame their pretty faces to their best advantage.

But Farida? No one, she knew, would be interested in her. She smiled at the distorted reflections she got back, now from the brass pot in her hands, as she thought back upon the events of her day. Then she remembered some details that she had purposely left out. Her expression darkened. She hadn't, for instance, described the clothes Mickey was wearing. Had she done so, Farida feared, she would not be permitted to go back to the house, regardless of how much she might be paid. Simply hearing of the skimpy top and the scandalous shorts would convince Salma-Bi that the house was a den of vice. She would declare that Farida would be corrupted and would forbid her to go there.

Not only that but Bahadur, Mary-*mem*'s cook, had spoken to Farida as she left to go home that evening. He was a thickset, tough-looking man, not an Indian at all, but from the mountain kingdom of Nepal. Nepalis were known for their honesty and trustworthiness, which made them favoured as domestic help in the homes of rich foreigners. Nevertheless, Farida had been afraid of him, when he had opened the door to her, on the first day of her work. He had seemed threatening, with his broad Mongolian features, brassy-brown skin and eyes buried deep within heavily creased lids. Even his hair had seemed threatening, cropped close so that it stood up straight like row upon row of black needles. He had frowned in her direction, seeming about to shout something rude, but had been thwarted by the presence, close at hand, of his employer, Mary-*mem*. So today, when he was the one to usher her out, Farida had felt the pulse beating in her throat, fearful of what he might say.

He had glanced around him as if checking to see whether the coast was clear, then indicated that he wished to walk down the stairs with her, to see her to the front gate. His manner stilled her fear, because he spoke to her in the tone of a friendly, well-intentioned adult. What he said, however, filled her with a different type of confusion: 'Better you don't work here, girlie!' he told her, in his Nepali-accented Hindi. 'Better for you! Hard to explain. The young *mem* – the white-haired one – she's not . . . *good*! Stay far from her.' Then he tapped the side of his head. 'Something wrong in here. Something loose.' He balled the fingers of his right hand into a thick, meaty fist which he rotated in a wobbly manner, suggesting a malfunctioning mechanical part.

Farida had not known what to say to these remarks. Bahadur, sensing from her expression that he was only confusing her, just shook his head once or twice before letting her go. She was glad that she did not need to fear him. On the contrary, by trying to warn her away, he was indicating his desire to be helpful. Yet she could not bring herself to take his advice. The job was her only chance of bettering her prospects, which had grown dim indeed ever since her mother had died.

Farida tightened her mouth as she put away the last of the utensils. Whatever happened, she was going to have to face the situation alone. She had set aside a small bowl of rice and dhal to eat once her chores were over. This she now took with her to the narrow landing outside the front door of her home. Settling in the corner between the edge of the landing and the wall behind her, she ate with quick, bird-like movements, using her fingers as a scoop, to convey food from the bowl to her mouth.

From where she sat, she could look out towards the modern and brightly lit areas of the city, where her employers lived. A deep orange glow, visible for miles around, hung suspended over the southern horizon like a festive umbrella.

Here, where Farida lived, electricity was such a rarity that most people depended on kerosene lamps inside their homes, even though they all had power lines snaking across the walls of their dwellings. Water was collected in buckets from the nearest standpipe and stored in earthen pots. Farida's father's neighbour had a toilet stall equipped with a functioning water connection. Both these facilities were used by the inhabitants in the vicinity, by paying a modest monthly fee. Inside Farida's home the kitchen area was at one end of the main room. A single tap in the kitchen produced a steady stream of water for one hour every morning and another hour every night.

All around her, Farida could hear the diesel generators powering the all-night workshops with a continuous thrumming din. Farida was so used to this sound, she had found the tranquil environment of her new workplace unnerving. For the whole of her first day there, she had felt as if she'd gone deaf, there was so little stimulation reaching her ears. It was only today, after three days of virtual silence, that she felt, for the first time, the relentless racket of her locality pressing in towards her thoughts.

After she had finished her meal and rinsed out her mouth, she returned to sit in her lookout, facing towards the south. She wondered what her employers were doing at that very moment. Were they eating? Or talking? Or sleeping? From what she had seen of their lives, they did no work. Mary's husband had a car with a driver. He went away in the morning, came back for lunch, then went out again. Was that enough to earn a good living, enough to afford a big apartment, like the one they had? Mary and Jenny did nothing at all aside from talking or going shopping or sitting around the table, eating and laughing. In Farida's world, by contrast, everyone squeezed every minute of the day bone dry for earning potential. Even so, all they could afford were these three small rooms, with its single tap.

Then there was that other thing: Mary's husband and the two women all sat together at mealtimes, just as if there were no differences between them! Farida knew this to be a thing specific to the fair-skinned foreigners, this mingling of the sexes as if they were on a par. For her, it was unthinkable to the point of repugnance. Ever since she had come of age, she was rarely alone even with her own father and never with any other men. She kept her head covered with her headscarf at all times. She was always conscious of the need to keep her voice low and her face politely averted. She never laughed out loud except in the company of children.

She could not understand how these women, Jenny-*mem* and Mary-*mem*, in other ways quite normal and familiar, could expose their legs and faces to the world without feeling shame. As for Mickey, Farida could only suppose that she was, as Bahadur hinted, mentally unstable to dress the way she did. And why did her mother not forcibly cover her up? Farida had never had a say in the choice of her clothing. She wore what she was given to wear. The idea of being wilful about her appearance or of behaving with anything less than absolute propriety was as unthinkable as the sun setting in the east.

How was it possible that the colour of skin could make such a difference to a person's behaviour? It was not a thought that had ever occurred to her before. This was the first time she was meeting foreigners, with their fair hair and large limbs, who seemed to breathe some very different air to herself. She knew of their world through occasional pictures in the pages of old magazines, recycled and used by vegetable sellers to wrap their produce in. She had seen foreign cinema posters and sometimes caught flashes of foreign programmes on the neighbour's TV. But the images she saw in those programmes were simply unreal. They were no different to the stories told at bedtime to children, to frighten or amuse them. It had never occurred to Farida that there could really be people whose lives and customs were so fundamentally different to her own as to make them practically unrecognizable as people at all.

A moth bumped into her forehead, reminding her that she must get some sleep, in order to wake up at four-thirty to collect the morning's ration of water. Stepping soundlessly through the room in which her father and stepmother slept, she entered the tiny, windowless space she shared with her four siblings. She unrolled the thin ticking on which she slept and lay down upon it. Cocooning herself against mosquitoes in a sheet that covered her from head to foot, she dropped like a stone into the well of sleep.

The next day, it was Mickey who opened the door to Farida. 'Come in,' she said, speaking in her clear, precise voice, about which there was, today, a certain inexplicable tension. 'Come this way, please —' Just behind Mickey, in the dining room, Mary and her sister stood by like spectators to a street play.

Farida's eyes were wide with uncertainty. Normally it was Bahadur who opened the door. She couldn't understand what could be the cause for the change. Mickey, meanwhile, was looking as peculiar as ever. She was wearing a short white T-shirt and tight white pants. Her face was made-up, as before, with shiny black lipstick and the thick black lines painted around her eyes.

She said to Farida, 'You're going to work in my room today. I've moved your things in there already.'

Then her tone softened as she asked, 'You . . . *do* understand me, yes?'

Farida dropped her eyes and said, 'Yes.'

Mickey led the way.

As she trailed after her, Farida heard Jenny say, 'I wish I could feel certain this was going to work out all right! D'you think I should follow along just to see that Mickey doesn't . . . try something funny?'

Mary paused before replying, 'No. Farida knows what she's about, even if Mickey doesn't.'

The guest room was vast, filled with books and small tables, a canopied bed, a grand glass-topped teak-wood desk and a whole wall covered with framed miniature paintings. Mickey had set Farida's work things out on the soft, deep-pile rug that glowed in the corner by the bay window. It was cold in here, colder even than the rest of the apartment.

Mickey said, 'I told Mummy it was inhuman to make you work outside in the burning heat. I couldn't stand for that. So she's allowed me to have you in here, if I promise not to disturb you. I'll sit here and read one of my books. You're to eat with us today. There's someone else coming to lunch, but I don't care. I told Mum that either you must eat at the table like everyone else or –' she shrugged, 'I won't let her give you any more work. I told her it was slave labour, what she was getting from you – at the prices she's paying you. I told her she should be ashamed not to pay you as much as you'd get if you were in England but . . . well, of course she wouldn't listen. She never does.' She sighed. 'Anyway, if there's anything you want, just ask me for it, OK?' With that, she sprawled across the double bed and opened her book.

Farida nodded, dumbly. She felt out of her depth and afraid to be alone with a girl who seemed so disrespectful towards her own mother. She hadn't understood everything Mickey had said, but gathered that she had been invited to lunch. Farida was too timid to point out that she had brought her own food and that besides, she was unwilling to eat with strangers, for fear of encountering forbidden substances in the meal. She decided, however, that she would face that hurdle when she came to it.

Four hours later, Bahadur knocked on the door to announce lunch. Mickey jumped up and said to Farida, 'Come on! I hope you're as hungry as I am —'

Farida took a deep breath and said, 'I . . . eat here.' She patted the floor and the little cloth bag in which she had brought her tiffin.

Mickey shook her head vehemently and grabbed her wrist. 'No, no — don't you see, it's important that you join us there — I insist —'

Not knowing what else to do, Farida got up and allowed herself to be led away, though with her whole spirit, she wanted nothing more than to be left alone.

All four adults had already settled down at their places when the girls arrived.

Andrew sat at the head of the table. Mary was on his right, facing the drawing room, while the Indian guest, Mr Neelkant, and Mickey's mother sat opposite her. There was an empty place next to Mary, which was meant to be Mickey's seat.

Mickey said, 'Farida will eat with us – she can have my seat.' She nudged Farida towards it. She drew back the only other available chair, which was at the foot of the table, facing her uncle. 'I'll sit here. Bahadur can set up my place for me. Please.'

Jenny began to say something but Mary cut in, quickly, 'Mickey, Farida – you haven't met –' she indicated the guest at the table '– Mr Neelkant. Andrew's colleague at the bank. Mr Neelkant – my niece Mickey and . . . of course, the young lady who has been working with us, whom I mentioned to you, Farida –'

Mr Neelkant smiled. 'Ah!' he said, 'Your little Muslim seamstress!' He was a genial man, in his late forties, with a full head of slick black hair and smooth, satiny skin. He addressed Farida directly, in Hindi, asking a question.

Farida sat with her head bowed, staring towards the bowl of cold consommé in front of her. She heard the question but took a few seconds to realize that it had been addressed to her. She answered in Hindi, not looking up, 'Yes.'

Mr Neelkant said to the others. 'Ah. I asked her if she understands English, and she has answered in the affirmative! An educated girl! A rarity in her community –' Since he and the other adults had already started on their soup, he took up his spoon again while saying to Farida, in English, 'Don't worry! This soup is safe for you to eat – it is not made from pork –' Then he glanced around the table at the others. 'It's a problem, you see, having such a guest at one's table . . . food prohibitions, you know! The curse of religious fanaticism.' He sipped from his spoon. 'I myself am not fastidious about such things. I am a Hindu, but unlike others of my religion, I eat beef.' He dabbed his mouth with his napkin. 'Of course our little friend there has probably never seen soup! Too bad for her – this one is excellent, by the way.'

Mary thanked him on Bahadur's behalf.

Then he continued. 'I must agree with you that your young seamstress is quite the little beauty! But I can tell you, her own people would be amazed to hear it. No doubt she is considered, in her family circles, very unattractive. Skin colour you know – we are very conscious of that in India and we – a dark people!' He was in a mood to be instructive. He pushed back the cuffs of his suit, exposing his wrists. 'See? I am the colour, let us say, of milky tea. That is considered acceptable. But our friend there, she is the colour of strong coffee! Not acceptable! Dark skin is associated with toiling under the hot sun, belonging to the labourer class. It is a sign of social deprivation. The lighter we Indians are, the more likely it is that we belong to the upper classes. Hence: despite her ideal features, your little seamstress will most likely not find a suitable husband –'

Mickey interrupted Mr Neelkant. Looking down the centre of the table to her uncle, she said, in a voice like a steel razor, 'Uncle Andrew? I think *your* guest is being very rude to *my* guest.'

Her uncle sucked in his breath and said, 'Mickey –'

Jenny said, 'Mickey!'

Mary said, 'And you are being rude to everybody, Mickey. Please apologize at once.'

In the pause before anything more could be said, Farida turned around in her seat so as to avoid pushing the chair back, stood up and walked out of the room. She went straight across the drawing room and through the glass doors to the veranda.

She continued to hear the others talking. Mickey, her voice suddenly childish, cried, 'Do you see that! You've insulted her! And after all the trouble I went to, to get her to sit with us!'

Mary said, 'Well, it was wrong of you. She was clearly uncomfortable. Surely you saw that?'

Andrew said, 'I agree with Mary. I think you should apologize –'

Jenny said, 'Yes! I insist! You're being horrid –'

Mickey responded hotly with, 'I don't understand how you can all – just go on pretending as if everything's all right! Just sitting here . . . eating and talking . . . as if . . . as if . . .' She seemed convulsed with emotions that left her speechless.

Jenny said, 'Oh darling! Please try and control yourself!'

Mickey, on the verge of tears, said, 'There's something wrong with all of you. You too, mother – you, especially! Or else you'd see it for what it is – Farida's really poor! I asked Bahadur and he told me – and you're just laughing and eating, and not even asking her to join us or anything! It's unthinkable! And making her work in the heat! And paying her absolutely nothing, almost! You'd never do that in England, you wouldn't dream of trying!'

Mr Neelkant said, in his suave voice, 'My dear young

lady! You must understand – Farida doesn't belong at this table, and she doesn't expect to. Her class of people, really, they're quite happy where they belong! They know their place . . . and we know ours. You're new to India, so this all must seem . . . strange! And wrong! But you'd get used to it in time. Everyone does.' He smiled in his oily way at the other adults. 'You'd begin to see that there's no other way to be and that we're all quite happy –'

Mickey said, 'Uncle Andrew – please! Make him stop! He can't get away with saying such awful things!'

But Andrew said, 'Don't be ridiculous, my dear –'

'You've told me yourself!' cried Mickey, '– that you think people here are cruel and unkind to one another – you believe that the Government is –'

Her uncle said, his voice crisp and cold, 'That will do, Mickey! I thought you were grown up enough to understand what I meant. But I was wrong, apparently . . . Maybe it would be best if you went to your room right away. Mary – ?' He expected his wife to arrange for Mickey's food to be taken in to her.

Mickey jumped to her feet. 'Oh!' she exclaimed, 'Oh! You're all just . . . horrid . . . old . . . racist . . .' She was gasping and crying at once. '*Pigs!*' And with this she ran from the room.

Farida had gone directly to Mickey's room, snatched up the top she had started working on before lunch and returned to the veranda. She sat down in her familiar position, under the potted plants, opened the bead cases and began working. Her needle flew back and forth, like a slender, steely bee, snatching up the beads three at a time, black, emerald green and scarlet, and flying back to the cloth between her hands, stinging it with violent jabs. Initially she wanted only her hardest colours, the darkest and shiniest. Then she opened all the cases and used the others too.

Hot, angry thoughts were tumbling through her mind. She could not remember being this furious before, as if she were filled to the brim with burning oil. She felt as if one layer of her skin had been ripped away, as she sat at that table. She didn't know whom to hate more: Mickey for having forced her to come out, or that disgusting guest, for having spoken to her and about her as if she were a lizard on the wall, with no wits or feelings.

She was certain she would be ordered out of the house. She knew it was inexcusably rude to have got up the way she had. She was amazed at her own daring. But what else could she have done? She could not imagine eating food that may have been prepared in ways forbidden by her religion. She could not understand how to use the armoury of utensils on either side of the plate. She could not endure to be in the presence of strange men who might stare at her unbidden, without her father's knowledge or permission.

In a few moments, the glass doors banged open and she thought her eviction orders were about to be delivered. Instead, however, it was Mickey who passed through them and straight to her room, sobbing. She did not look in Farida's direction and Farida did not look up in hers. Ten minutes later, Bahadur took the same route, carrying a tray of food in to Mickey. Farida saw him from the corner of her eye, but did not lift her face up. It seemed to her that he paused, as he came out of the room, and may have been expecting her to look up and catch his eye, but since she didn't oblige him, she couldn't be sure.

At the moment he opened the bedroom door, she had heard the sound of stormy crying from within. She could not fathom what reason the other girl had for being unhappy. Nevertheless, she felt a childish satisfaction in the thought that Mickey, despite all her freedoms and privileges, had been the one to lose her composure.

Presently, she heard the sound of the bedroom door opening again. Though she didn't look up, she knew that Mickey had emerged once more. She came towards Farida in her bare feet, then paused a long moment before folding herself down so that she was also sitting on Farida's mat. For a while, the two of them sat thus, Farida with her flying needle and Mickey with her silence.

From the corner of her eye, Farida saw that Mickey had apparently washed her face clear of make-up. The lids of her eyes were pink and swollen from crying. She was calm, however. Calmer than she'd been before lunch.

When the right moment came, Farida paused in her beading and looked up. Mickey bent forwards to examine the embroidered cloth and said, 'That really is amazing work.' Farida gave it to her to hold, and she placed it against herself, seeing that it would become a heavily decorated black halter-neck top. 'Is it for me?'

Farida looked at her own handiwork as if seeing it for the first time. The pattern, if it could be called that, was like none she had ever made before. It was a higgledy-piggledy arrangement composed of all the beads in her collection, yet it looked, in an unlikely way, harmonious. It was the kind of pattern her stepmother would have instantly destroyed, seeing the work of the Twisted One in its reckless asymmetry.

But who was there to deny that asymmetry may, after all, be the higher pattern? It was the Supreme Creator who had fashioned mortal beings in a range of different colours, shapes and sizes. Like assorted beads. Yet the same air was threaded equally through all, stitching every one into the cloth of reality with a randomness that was, in its own way, beautiful. If He, in all His perfection, were capable of such pranks, well then! She, Farida, need have no fear!

She would simply avoid telling Salma-Bi anything about the new design.

Retrieving the cloth from Mickey's hands, Farida said in English, 'Yes. For you. You like? You want, I teach you? Is easy!'

'Yes,' said Mickey, settling down more comfortably on the mat, 'yes, I'd like!'

Manjula Padmanabhan, born in 1953, is a full-time writer and artist. She has published five books including Hot Death, Cold Soup, *a collection of short stories and* Harvest, *a play, which won the 1997 Onassis Award. For several years she drew 'Suki', a daily comic strip in the* Pioneer, *a newspaper in New Delhi. Manjula has illustrated over twenty books for children, including her own fifth book,* Mouse Attack.

Cousins

by Merav Alazraki

A story set in Israel and the West Bank

Ofir lived on Kibbutz Kabri in western Galilee. It was a rural communal settlement, situated on the western edge of the mountains of northern Israel, overlooking the Mediterranean. The fertile valley that stretched almost all the way to the sea was full of the kibbutz's plantations and fields with their different crops – banana, mango, avocado, orange orchards and others. Ofir loved going with his father when he went to work in the fields, especially when it was time for banana harvesting. It was by far his favourite work, a real man's work that he could not do yet. But he loved watching his father cutting off the heavy banana tree stalks with his big machete. Ofir would help carry the stalks to the tractor. They were always very heavy, with more than twenty bananas a stalk.

The best part of the day was break time when the farmworkers Mahmoud, Ahmed and Munir would invite Ofir to join them. They would squat down, feet

177

flat on the ground, and take out large pitta breads, *laba'ne*, *za'atar* and olive oil. The sour cheese with the spice was a delicious combination Ofir couldn't resist even though he would end up with oily hands and a face full of white streaks from the dried cheese. When they'd finished eating, the three would lean on tree branches, shaded by bananas, and enjoy the cool western breeze with its scent of the Mediterranean. Then they would take their *narghile* out and start smoking the special pipe with the scented tobacco. The smoke had such a sweet flavour and fragrance that once Ofir begged to try it out.

'Abu Ofir,' the three men cried out to his father, 'what do you think?'

They never called his dad by his name, Shlomo, like everyone else, always Abu Ofir, father of Ofir. It made Ofir feel important and warm inside. And his dad laughed and said, 'What is it today? Is it safe?'

'Just some apple tobacco,' came the answer and Ofir was given the golden-plated end of the red tube. He put it to his mouth and sucked. The water in the green glass bubbled and the tobacco scorched the aluminium foil that covered the ceramic top of the *narghile*. The taste filled Ofir's mouth, and his senses grew slightly numb as he enjoyed the apple flavour inside him and the smell around him.

'Yalla,' Shlomo said to them after a while, 'yalla, to work.'

Rafiq was born in Dura Al-Qari'a, a quiet rural village north of Jerusalem. Among the mountains, valleys and hills, Rafiq's family's lands bore many olive groves. Rafiq attended his first olive harvesting when he was less than one year old, and could remember running around the trees while the olive picking was going on. The whole family was there, his mother, father, two sisters and three brothers. He was the youngest in his family and suffered the usual brotherly abuse and sisterly care, or over care, so sometimes he tried to hide. He would try to find a tree with the biggest trunk and hide behind it. While he was hiding he would explore the tree trunk, each of them unique with its own twists and turns. The older the olive tree was, the bigger its trunk, and the more kinks and curves the trunk had. Like snakes of different sizes winding and spiralling around each other, intertwining, sometimes bulging out, sometimes creating holes, meeting, then separating into the different branches. Rafiq would pretend to be blind like Uncle Yusuf and feel the tree with his hands.

From their field they could see the military outpost overlooking them. Each time Rafiq's mother happened to look up at the outpost she wished for the ruin of the soldiers' houses in a juicy curse. Rafiq couldn't understand why. He always wanted to be a soldier just like them, carrying a big gun and riding an army jeep with the long antennae in the back. The soldiers looked so strong, and everybody was afraid of them. Not Rafiq, though. He defied his parents and talked to them; and the soldiers sometimes gave him sweets. The last time he accepted sweets from the soldiers was after one particular harvesting and the oil pressing, a few days before Eyal came to buy their oil.

Rafiq saw Eyal's truck approaching, and he ran inside to tell his father, Abu Jamal, who went outside to greet him.

'Come, enter.' Abu Jamal spoke to Eyal in Arabic.

Eyal went in and sat in their living room in the place Abu Jamal pointed to.

'Suha,' Abu Jamal called to his wife, 'we have a guest. Some tea and sweets.'

'Abu Jamal, Umm Jamal,' Eyal said once Suha brought the bronze tray laden with tea in clear tall glasses and the best sweets. She had prepared them only that morning. 'I bring you clothes after my family,' said Eyal, trying out his Arabic. He pushed forwards a big bag, and added something in Hebrew that Rafiq couldn't understand.

'No, no, I don't mind at all, I'm not insulted, thank you,' Rafiq's father said and then also continued in Hebrew.

Once Rafiq's father and Eyal finally went outside to complete their business, Rafiq's curiosity overcame him and he started checking the bag. No one was in the living room and he had time to go over the contents slowly. He took out the clothes one at a time. A light yellow girl's dress, khaki shorts that were much too big, a pair of cartooned cotton pyjamas. He chose the clothes that might fit him and put them aside, when he suddenly noticed one shirt, a sports jersey, a real one, a hot red Liverpool Ian Rush jersey. It was slightly big on Rafiq, but he didn't mind. He put it on and fetched his football, forgetting all about the bag and the clothes. He liked Rush because he had a moustache just like his father and Jamal, his big brother. He started to bounce the football on his knee, his eyes glistening with joy.

'You let him hang out with those dirty Arabs again,' Ofir's mother accused her husband.

'Come on, Anat, we've been through this before. What's the harm? They're nice people.' Shlomo resisted her accusation weakly.

'Nice?' Anat bawled. 'Until you turn your back to them, that is. That's when they stab you. Right then.'

'Look.' Shlomo showed her a jar filled with white cheese balls suspended in olive oil. 'Munir even brought us some *laba'ne* his wife made. He knows how much Ofir loves it.'

'It's probably poisoned,' Anat snorted.

'It's not poisoned, Mammi,' Ofir tried to reassure her. 'I had some today and I feel fine.'

Anat stroked her son's hair and knelt on the floor so that she was eye level with him. 'Promise me that you will be careful around them,' she said firmly, holding his eyes with hers until he could no longer bear her gaze and turned his eyes away.

He didn't like that piercing look she had. Something about it made him afraid. Even at his young age he could feel the hatred, the fear, the loathing. 'OK, OK.' He tried to get away from his mother's arms. 'I'll be careful.' He struggled out of her grasp at last and said, 'But why do you hate them?'

''Because they are murderous terrorists and . . .'

She was going to add something else but her husband cut her off. 'Now is not the time. He is too young.'

'Now is the perfect time,' said Anat bitterly. 'He should know who he's dealing with if you're going to let him hang around with them. Come, sit,' she said to Ofir, getting herself under control. She motioned to Ofir to sit on the couch. He looked up at his mother as she remained standing and paced back and forth a few times, clearly thinking of the best way to tell her story.

'Remember the pictures of Auntie Ayelet in Grandma's house?' she said after a while.

Ofir nodded.

'Well,' Anat said, a determined expression on her face. Shlomo was looking at his wife in a way that Ofir had seen before, usually when he'd been sick and his father was taking care of him. It was a look that combined love and concern. Ofir felt the tension and moved to the edge of the couch, feet dangling in the air, swinging back and forth in nervous anticipation and with fear as to what he was about to hear.

'Well,' Anat started again, her own voice breaking, 'you see, before you were born, when Ayelet was in eleventh grade, she went on a field trip with her class. They went to a school in Ma'alot to sleep there overnight.'

'Ma'alot? Where Uncle Dov lives?'

'Yes.' Anat answered in a choked voice. She walked to another sofa and sat down. She seemed to be thinking as her eyes were shut and her face contorted.

Ofir slid off the couch and went over to his mother. He put his little hand on her leg.

Anat picked Ofir up and hugged him. She held him

tight and whispered, 'My baby,' in his ear. She sat him on her lap and went on with her story. 'Three Arab terrorists came to the school and shot many students.' She was speaking in a soft voice, caressing her son. 'And Ayelet was one of the many they shot. Most of them schoolgirls.' Anat's expression was distant, as if she were remembering her dead sister. Shlomo walked over to them, stood above his wife and held her hand.

'Why did they shoot Ayelet?' said Ofir, breaking the adults' silence. 'Was she a bad girl?'

'No, baby,' said Anat. Her tears were slowly making a path down her cheeks. 'She was a fantastic girl. She was very smart and very beautiful.' Anat stopped and her husband squeezed her shoulder. 'She was so funny . . .' Anat's last attempt to describe her sister was drowned in her quiet weeping.

'They were bad men, son,' Shlomo said to Ofir, trying to explain something he himself could not understand.

'They were not men,' said Anat, her voice full of anger. 'They were animals. They're all animals, murderous cowards. All of them.'

There was sadness in her voice too, and Ofir found it hard to grasp how she could feel both things at once. He still didn't understand completely what had happened, or why.

'It's not enough that my mother lost all her family at the hands of the Nazis in the Holocaust,' Anat said. 'She then had to lose her daughter to Arab terrorists here, in the country that was supposed to give her safety, comfort and relief.'

'But Mahmoud and Munir and Ahmed are good Arabs, aren't they?' said Ofir.

'The only good Arab is a dead Arab,' Anat snapped at her own son. But then she softened and leaned her head on Shlomo. 'I'm sorry,' she said, her tears flowing again.

'What's that you're wearing?'

'It's a Liverpool shirt,' said Rafiq. 'From the clothes Eyal brought us.' Rafiq was still bouncing the football.

Abu Jamal quickly went up to his son. Rafiq took a few steps back, recognizing anger in his father's eyes. He crouched as his father caught him, tore the shirt off him, put all the clothes back in the bag, grabbed both the bag and Rafiq and led him outside.

'What's wrong? What did I do?' Rafiq was shouting the whole time. He was struggling to loosen his father's grip and free himself to no avail.

Suha heard her son's screams and came out to see what was wrong. She watched her husband silently.

'Stay here!' Abu Jamal barked at his son as he got the big red plastic gasoline container from the other side of the yard.

Rafiq was horrified. He'd never seen his father so angry in his life, and he still didn't know what he'd done wrong. His father was always a happy, smiling man, but now his mouth was twisted, his eyes bulging in rage. Suha walked to Rafiq and put her hand on his shoulder. Rafiq turned to look at her, and saw instantly that she wasn't mad at him. There was a look of sadness in her eyes instead.

Abu Jamal poured gasoline on the clothes and then

set them on fire. He spat on them for good measure and said, 'This is what you do with contaminated clothes from Zionists. Don't you ever accept anything from those murderous animals. You hear?' He shook his son's shoulders.

Rafiq nodded in fear.

'Adel, the boy doesn't understand, you're scaring him. You should explain.'

Abu Jamal looked at his wife, and then at his frightened son. 'You're right,' he said. 'It's time he understood who these Jews are.' He bent down so that he could see into Rafiq's eyes. 'Remember I told you about the *naqba*? The disaster when the Zionists declared their state and it became Israel and they took our lands?'

Rafiq nodded.

'This filthy pig, Eyal, lives on our land, the land taken from Uncle Yusuf.'

'But Uncle Yusuf lives with us,' said Rafiq, confused. 'He has no land.'

'Because *they* took it,' said his father. Abu Jamal composed himself and started explaining again more quietly this time. 'Uncle Yusuf still has the key to the house he had in Daniyal. They built a kibbutz there called Kfar Daniel instead, and they destroyed Uncle Yusuf's home.'

Rafiq remembered seeing the key his father was telling him about. Uncle Yusuf had shown it to Rafiq on many occasions, telling him it was the key to his house, but Rafiq never understood. The old wrought-iron key didn't look at all like the key to their house.

'Is that why Uncle Yusuf is blind?' Rafiq said, half remembering something else he'd overheard.

Abu Jamal looked at his son, and then at his wife. She smiled in reassurance. 'Well, one day, when you were just a baby,' said Abu Jamal, 'the Zionists came to take us in the middle of the night. I was so worried about you.' He paused and stroked his son's head. 'The men of the family went outside to plead with the soldiers to take them quietly and leave the rest of the house in peace, but it didn't help. The soldiers were looking for a terrorist, they said, and thought that we were hiding him in the house. So they pushed us out of the way, hitting me in my leg and Uncle Yusuf in the head. That's what caused his blindness. Then they went in the house and broke most of the furniture in their search. They hit your brother Jamal with a club and broke his hand, which is why it's twisted. But you know what?' Abu Jamal asked his son.

Rafiq waited for his father to continue, his heart beating.

Abu Jamal's eyes glistened as he looked at his son. 'You,' he said, holding his son's shoulders just below the hands of Suha. 'You never woke up. You slept through the whole thing. And I looked at your sweet peaceful face and the memory of it gave me strength while I was in prison. I could see you in my head as you were, happy and smiling in your mother's arms, your eyes closed.'

Suha lowered her hands to touch her husband's. 'That's when I knew that there is always hope, and that they can't take everything away from us.'

Rafiq felt strangely proud of the idea that his father had drawn strength from him, that somehow he had saved his father in prison. He wasn't sure he understood it yet, but it made him feel good. 'What happened then?' He desperately wanted to hear the end of the story.

'Me and Jamal were taken in for no reason. The conditions were terrible, and I was so worried about all of you. But then after a week they released me. Although they kept Jamal for three years.' Abu Jamal paused. 'That's why you should never forget who these Israelis are and what they did to your people and family.'

'But Eyal is nice, and that soldier that gave me the sweets is nice. Not all Jews are bad, are they?'

'No, not all Jews are bad,' his father said through clenched teeth. 'I don't mind the ones that don't live in our country.' He got up and looked west. Israel lay there, on the horizon. 'One day we will drive them all into the sea and reclaim our land,' he said in a quiet voice. 'Just wait and see. They will either die or flee.'

Ofir was on patrol, bringing up the rear. He hated being in the rear, a vulnerable position. He ran two steps, turned around and looked behind him, pointing his gun back the way they'd come. A woman was looking at him from a window on the second floor of the building behind him and to the side. She was wearing a white head-covering. Ofir looked at her pointing his gun, but she looked at him in defiance. Three windows to her left and one floor up, a child was looking at Ofir. When the child thought Ofir's attention was elsewhere he pointed his finger, pretending to shoot him. Of course Ofir noticed, but he ignored it and turned and continued to run.

It was high noon and the refugee camp reeked. Ofir cynically thought the stench was the only colourful thing in this place. The rest was grey – the buildings, the roads, the tents, the alleys – everything. There was a curfew, but he could still hear some children playing in an alley not far from the patrol route.

'Hold it!' Ofir heard a distant shout. It sounded like his company's commander's voice, speaking in Arabic.

Ofir ran faster, stopping every six or ten steps to check the rear. When he reached the rest of the company he saw the commander, Captain Gil, talking to an old man in a long grey dress. Ofir did not speak much Arabic, but he understood what the old man was saying.

'I'm just trying to . . .'

Gil pointed his gun straight at the man's face. 'Inside! Curfew!' he shouted.

The man gave Gil a loathing look. He opened his mouth to speak again, but then he sighed heavily. He turned and went into the building, disappearing in the darkness.

Ofir kept looking around, his back against the wall, his gun pointing outwards. A little girl peered from a window just across from him. Her curly hair was fair, her blue eyes fearful, her colourful dress so faded, looking as grey as the rest. Ofir tried to smile at her, but her mother quickly closed the blinds. Ofir smiled wryly to himself. He knew the kind of stories they'd been teaching them, just as the Nazis had used complete fabrication like *The Protocols of the Elders of Zion* to justify their hatred. For a moment Ofir found himself wondering what lies he might have been told, what myths he had grown up on that were not true. But he drove the thoughts from his mind. He had to maintain alertness in order to survive in this hostile environment. He had had enough of this godforsaken place. Ofir tried to cheer himself up with the thought of going home that evening. Home, after being in the territories for three long weeks. Home to his mother's cooking and his girlfriend's sweet smile.

'Hold it! Stop! Don't move!' He heard Gil's shouting again. Ofir wasn't entirely sure what was going on at the front of the patrol. All the troops speeded up to minimize the gap. But before Ofir could see Gil, he heard the gunfire. When he did see Gil, he was sitting down and Ofir realized that gunfire was coming at them from several directions. They were cornered, try-ing to hide behind a building, occasionally firing back at the shooters. Gil was wounded, but not badly. Ofir looked around him. His hands were shaking as he tried to steady his grip on his gun, pointing it here and there in nervousness. Suddenly he heard a yell behind him and he crouched, waiting for a bullet to hit him any moment, terrified. He whirled round and fired only to see a little boy, about three or four and dressed in dirty rags, his face covered in dirt and tears, his nose running. The boy wasn't hit but he was standing near the entrance of a building in the alley, crying in fear. Ofir heard another yell, coming not from the boy, but from somewhere beyond him. There was someone else, standing in the opposite building.

'Hold it!' Ofir called out in his broken Arabic to whoever was hiding in the darkness, a darkness created by the sharp contrast of the bright sunlight outside with the shadows of the covered entrance.

A shout was directed at him, then at the child. Words he didn't understand.

Was it a woman? 'Stop!' Ofir repeated, almost pleading now, his voice betraying the immense dread he felt.

Another shout came out of the entrance. The boy was still crying, and just as Ofir saw a figure coming out of the darkness, he heard shots. He pulled the trigger and sprayed the entrance with bullets, noticing as he did so a figure falling down. He was relieved that his training had saved him. The little boy's cries stopped, as did the gunfire, and for a moment all was quiet.

Ofir went over and looked down at the figure in the dirt. It was a woman, a heavily pregnant woman, blood pulsing out of her chest and neck. The boy started crying again, louder, and kept saying one word, over and over again. This time Ofir understood. It was a universal word, wasn't it? *Mother.*

A moment later Ofir heard the command to continue and blindly followed it. He closed his mind, did what his instincts and training told him, followed the man in front numbly.

It was eleven in the evening. Complete darkness covered Rafiq and his friends in this moonless night as they climbed up the hill. His cell friends were like a second family to him. They had lost three so far. Two in fights with the 'Israeli' army and one a *shahid*, a martyr, who had blown himself up killing nine Israelis! Rafiq thought how lucky his friend was to sacrifice himself in the name of the cause, killing so many and wounding even more – all potential soldiers of the Zionist terrorists who were killing his people day after day.

Rafiq missed his own family. He hadn't seen them for almost a month, as he couldn't live with his parents any more. He had taken part in too many operations targeting soldiers, settlers and Israelis, and he had become a wanted man. He and his friends moved around all over the city, and the surrounding villages and camps, sleeping in different places every few nights.

They finally reached the kibbutz and the point in the fence that had been cut ahead of time by a co-conspirator who worked there. They sneaked through silently and went to the closest house. There were three of them, Rafiq and two others, a good number for such an operation. Soon they would kill some Zionists, Rafiq thought. He was excited, but there was that other feeling too, the misgiving he sometimes had about killing. But then why should he care? These were murderous animals, not human beings.

They reached the door of the house, their weapons ready. Hasan started fiddling with the lock, while Ahmed and Rafiq stood on either side, their backs against the wall, watching for any movement on the street. All was quiet. Rafiq could see the guard at the watchtower shining the searchlight around the kibbutz.

The beam moved over the fence, but the guard didn't spot the hole.

Hasan mumbled something Rafiq couldn't understand, but he saw Ahmed suddenly go tense. Hasan took a few steps back and shot at the lock. From then on the noise was appalling. Everything happened so fast that Rafiq had no time to think. They kicked the door in and saw a woman running through the corridor and into a room, slamming the door behind her. Before they had time to adjust to the lighting in the house, a man came out of another room with a small handgun. He shot once, and Rafiq could feel the bullet pass near him. Ahmed, who was in front, shot the man down, then walked over and shot him through the head, a guaranteed kill. They could hear screaming coming from the room the woman had run into. Hasan told them to spread out and see if there were any more people in the house. While Rafiq was doing that, he could hear the woman speaking in Hebrew inside the closed room, trying to quieten some kids. At least one of the children was crying, but the sound was suddenly stifled, as if someone had put a hand over the child's mouth.

Ahmed and Rafiq returned within ten seconds, and said that the rest of the place was empty. They could still hear occasional whispers from the closed room. The kibbutz siren was sounding now too, and there were shouts outside. Hasan didn't hesitate. He kicked the room door open. Rafiq saw a little boy, nine or ten years old, on the window sill, about to jump out. The woman was helping him, and a small girl with black hair and big brown eyes was beside her holding her mother's nightie. The woman moved quickly, trying to shield her son with her own body, but Hasan was quicker and shot the boy down. He turned his gun on the woman who leaned over her daughter, trying to cover as much of her as she could. Rafiq could see the horror and fear in her face.

'No,' Rafiq heard her saying. The word was almost identical in Hebrew and Arabic, and Rafiq had no problem understanding. 'Please.'

Hasan and Ahmed ignored her. She was still talking in Hebrew when they shot her. She fell on her daughter who was too frightened to even cry. Hasan mumbled in frustration and started shooting the woman again and again until the bullets penetrated her shielding body and her daughter was hit.

Then all was quiet in the house once more. The only noise came from the outside. Everything had happened in a few moments and the soldiers outside still had no idea which house was in trouble. Before they left, Rafiq looked back. Out of the melange of bodies his eyes were drawn to the black hair of the little girl sprawled on the floor beneath her mother. It was spread out over the only part of the floor not covered in blood.

Rafiq started running towards the fence, and then crawled past it. There were some shots but Rafiq hardly noticed them. He just kept running and running. He wanted to run straight home and curl up in his bed, but he knew that would endanger his family, and besides, the commander would want a briefing. Rafiq wasn't sure how long he ran, but at some point he heard

Hasan's voice calling him. He stopped and looked around, as if just waking up from sleeping too long, dazed and confused. Hasan was some thirty metres behind him.

'Where's Ahmed?' was the first thing Rafiq asked when Hasan reached him.

'He was gunned down back in the kibbutz. A martyr. Where's your gun?'

Rafiq didn't know. He hadn't realized that he'd lost his gun. When did he drop it? Or did he throw it away? He wasn't sure. 'It was jammed so I threw it away.' It was a lie but he had to say something.

Hasan looked at him, a smug expression on his face. 'Job well done,' he said and put his arm around Rafiq. 'Let's go and report.'

Rafiq thought that he was going to throw up. He wasn't sorry for Ahmed. In fact, he almost wished the same had happened to Hasan and himself. He didn't know how long he could bear his 'friend' touching him. Suddenly he felt that he was doomed.

Tamara walked into Ofir's room. He was curled up in the corner with only his underwear on. His dusty uniform was thrown on the other side of the floor, covering the M-16.

'Ofir,' she whispered.

Ofir didn't look at her. He heard her closing the door and coming towards him. She sat on the floor and put her arms around him. He shivered at her touch.

'I came as soon as your mother called me,' she said quietly. She paused for a while and Ofir knew that she was trying to gauge his feelings. 'You need to sleep,' she said at last, helping Ofir up and leading him to the bed. Ofir gave in to her, let himself be led, and lay down. Tamara covered him in the light blanket appropriate for the hot weather. She leaned over and hugged him softly. Tamara's gentleness soothed Ofir's broken soul, and he put his arms around her. After a moment or two, he started to weep, quietly. She stroked his head and let him sob until he fell asleep.

'I am not going back,' Ofir told her when he woke up.

'You can't not go back. What do you mean? Become a deserter?'

'No,' he said calmly. 'I will go back to the army. I believe in protecting my country, I am a proud Israeli. But I won't go back to the territories.'

'But why? What happened?' She was almost afraid to hear his answer.

Ofir said nothing for a while. Then he sighed quietly and said, 'I killed a woman.' He felt relieved now he'd told Tamara. He looked in her eyes, searching for absolution there. He buried his face in her neck and shoulder as shame overcame him. 'I'm a murderer.' He whispered so she almost couldn't hear him.

Tamara pulled his head up and looked at him intently, trying to convince him with her eyes that he was forgiven. 'But it was in the heat of battle, you were defending yourself and your country.'

'Killing a pregnant woman trying to reach her son is not defending my country,' he said quietly. 'It's because I want to defend my country, it's because I'm a Zionist, because I love Israel and believe in the Jewish state that I will not go back there. We have no business being there. It is not Israel.' Suddenly he felt stronger. He knew in his heart this was right. He knew he would have to carry the guilt of what he had done for the rest of his life with him.

'They will put you in jail,' Tamara said, kissing him softly.

Ofir felt her warmth. He saw the love in her beautiful eyes. 'I know,' he said, and kissed her back.

Rafiq wasn't sure how long the report took, or where he was sent to afterwards. They moved him again to a different house. He went through the motions, he ate, bathed, shaved, but he almost never slept. He thought that three days had passed when his father came to visit.

'Ahlan, Abu Jamal,' he heard the host say. 'Rafiq is here.'

Rafiq was alone in a corner of the living room when they entered. He blinked at the open door and saw the two dark figures at the entrance. When they closed the door, he recognized his father. He got up and went to him. Once he got close he saw all the love and concern in his father's face as he carefully examined his son and assessed his condition. His arms were held out wide, and Rafiq jumped into his arms and started weeping quietly so that no one would notice. Only his father felt the uncontrollable sobs and hid them with his arms.

'I'm taking you home, my son.'

'They won't let you. It's too dangerous for you and for me. They're afraid that if I get caught I'll talk.'

'Don't worry, I have it all figured out. I talked to Abu Ziyad. He agreed.'

Rafiq let his father lead him through the curfew and soldiers and checkpoints. They finally got to a relative's house. All his family was there, and they all kissed him and hugged him and blessed him. It wasn't a hero's welcome, although some of the younger kids did look at him in awe. It was a welcome for a long lost family member, someone they worried about. His mother held him for a long time and cried.

'Yalla, Suha, let the boy be.' His father helped Rafiq to release himself from his mother's grasp and motioned Rafiq to follow him. He took Rafiq to a secret door behind which was a small room. 'You can hide here,' he told his son, giving him a searching look.

Rafiq sat down on the mattress they had put out for him on the floor. His father sat next to him. They didn't speak, and for a while the silence said more than words could.

At long last Rafiq stirred and turned to his father. 'Do you know what I did?' he said, his voice shaking, his eyes dry. No tears could make up for what he had done. Of that he was absolutely sure.

Abu Jamal wanted to devour his son's pain. He took his son's hand in his. 'There is no god but the One God,' Abu Jamal said quietly to himself. He then turned to his son. 'I know,' he said. After a pause he added, 'But it wasn't you, it was Hasan.'

'Oh, what difference does it make? I knew what we

were going to do, only I didn't realize that they can look so much like us.' He stared into his father's eyes, searching for some absolution, something to release him from his pain. 'You know,' he said, his voice suddenly choked, 'she looked just like Nawal.' Nawal was his cousin, daughter of his father's brother. 'The same dark hair and brown eyes.'

Abu Jamal held his son's hand, trying to absorb some of the agony. He had no words of wisdom to offer.

'How can I look at my cousin now? Knowing I killed someone who could have been her? She looked so much like her.'

Abu Jamal took out his *subha*, rosary. He put it in his son's hand. 'Pray to God,' he said, 'say his names and recite the Koran.' He turned and picked up a black book from the table. 'Read the Koran. It will give you solace. The words of the Prophet, praise be upon him, will help you.'

Rafiq looked at his father. 'It's the Koran they use to justify what I did.'

'Black and wicked souls would find callous meaning in everything. Those souls that are hurt and confused cannot interpret the Prophet's words correctly. But you will read it, and find your own meaning, and that meaning will be true to you, and it will give you comfort, my son.'

Rafiq put the *subha* in his pocket and took the book. 'In the Name of Allah, the Most Gracious, the most Merciful,' he said quietly as he opened the holy book at a marked page. 'Our Lord! Perfect our light for us and forgive us our sins, for verily You have power over all things.' He read in silence the holy words and felt lighter than he had felt for days.

'Cousins' is Merav's first published work of fiction. She was born in Israel and was deeply affected by the Palestinian and Israeli conflict. Merav currently resides in Toronto, Canada.

Justice

by Rasheda Ashanti Malcolm

A story set in present-day Jamaica and London

I've always looked older than my age. When I was twelve and three-quarters, almost thirteen years of age, I towered over most of my friends. That's because I'm tall and thin, and being thin made me look even taller. I was taller than most of the boys in my class, except of course Mikey Collins who was a giant and stood out in a crowd. I often wondered what he would look like when he became a man, but because I was leaving Jamaica to live abroad, I guessed I would never find out.

It wasn't my idea to come and live in this foreign place. It wasn't even Aunt Clara's, who I'd lived with all my life. My mother made that decision; a woman I'd never met or at least I couldn't remember ever meeting.

During that summer holiday, with no homework or assignments to worry about, I had more time to think about my coming departure from Jamaica to the big unknown foreign country where my mother lived. A place everyone called London-Foreign. What I knew about that place was what Aunt Clara taught me from stories, books and the BBC World Service. Aunt Clara didn't own a television and neither did she want to; she said it only encouraged corruption and idleness. We would always listen to the World Service though, because they spoke so proper and Aunt Clara said it was a good influence for me.

I knew all about the big clock called Big Ben and the tower where they used to hang the kings and queens. I'd heard about the huge palace where the real queen lived and knew that the prime minister lived at Number 10 down the road from the queen. Yes, sir, I knew a lot, but I was still afraid, and I wasn't looking forward to going but I didn't know why.

'Justice, yuh really going to London-Foreign to live?' Kelly, my best friend in the whole of the world, asked me as we walked along the banks of Green River, the river that runs through the little town where I lived. I saw one of them wild hares scuttling into the bushes and I thought to chase it, then remembered Kelly saying them things were very childish now we were near teenagers, so I stopped myself.

'Yeah,' I replied, but I was reluctant and changed the subject quickly. 'Yuh want a swimming race?' I ran slightly ahead, kicking off my sandals before jumping on to a smooth piece of flat rock embedded by the edge of the river. I jogged on the spot, waiting for her to catch up.

'How long yuh staying in London-Foreign?' Kelly persisted, when she finally caught up.

'I don't know.' I shrugged my shoulders. Aunt Clara said I must stop doing that because it was bad manners but I couldn't help it, it was kind of natural – I did it without even thinking about it.

'Ma says yuh not coming back. Yuh're going to live in a country far across the clouds where ice falls from the sky.' Kelly finished dramatically, as she always did, but she sure looked concerned and I was too – ice falling from the sky? I'd never heard about that on the World Service!

'Real ice?' I knew I sounded incredulous, but I was visualizing great chunks of ice falling from the sky, and people dodging to miss them and wondering if it was real.

'Yes.' Kelly sounded sure. 'And my ma says yuh have to wear four and five sweaters.'

I was bewildered. I couldn't imagine anything cold enough to make wearing four or five sweaters possible. Even when it rained in Alexander Town, where we lived, you didn't need a sweater. Even late at night when the sun went down, or early in the morning when the trees and the grass were wet with dew, you only needed one sweater. And Kerry hadn't finished with her tales of horror about London-Foreign.

'Yuh'll be flying in the plane for about two hundred hours, it's a long, long way away . . . it's about twenty thousand miles across the sky.'

'Are yuh sure?' I asked her because I thought I remembered the World Service saying something like eight thousand miles, but she nodded her head and I wasn't sure enough to disagree.

'Is that more than twenty thousand acres?' I asked, thinking about the big plantation Mr Hampshire owned along with lots of holiday cottages in Alexander Town. Aunt Clara said he had twelve acres, and it was far enough from one end of his twelve acres to the other. Twenty thousand was the end of the earth!

'Plenty more,' Kelly confirmed.

I put on my sandals, knowing no swimming was going to take place that day. I walked away from the riverbank and sat on the soft green grass around it. I sat with my knees to my chest and my arms resting on them. I looked thoughtfully into space. I didn't want Kelly knowing how much she was scaring me. Kelly sat close to me, resting her head on my arm.

'Are yuh scared?' she asked.

'Of what?' I played brave.

'I don't know.' She raised her head to look at me and I knew it was just to see if I was as brave as I sounded.

'It seems stupid to be frighten' of what yuh don't know,' I said.

It went all quiet. Kelly followed my stare towards the skies. 'The people have white faces too.'

'Huh?' I quizzed.

'The people in London-Foreign, they have white faces like Mr Hampshire. I'm so glad it's yuh going and not me. I hear if yuh stare too long at their white faces, yuh get sick and can even drop dead.'

'Is that true?' I wasn't convinced, but I felt terrified inside. Kelly was smaller than me but she had enough breasts to put in a bra, which I didn't, so that meant she knew what she was talking about, right?

'Yuh bet it's true. Mr Hampshire is different. He loves black people, that's why he got a black wife, but Ma says most of them whiteys hate black people, yuh mustn't turn yuh back on one,' Kelly warned.

On the three-mile walk back to my house, I made up my mind to tell Aunt Clara that I wouldn't be going to that foreign place and no one could make me. I would run away if they tried. I got home just as Master Percy was leaving. This ancient-looking man with a head full of silver hair always delivered the water on a Tuesday evening and returned at the same time the following week to fill Aunt Clara's water tank at the back of the house. If we ran out of water before then, it was one of my chores to take the buckets and walk half a mile to the village pipe which was for people who couldn't afford to have water delivered to their house. Aunt Clara said that my mother in London-Foreign wanted to buy us a new house with pipes that would bring the water into the taps, but she said she was born in this one and it was where she wanted to die. Anyway, I didn't like to think about Aunt Clara dying.

'Good evening, Justice. Looking forward to Foreign?'

That was all I needed, a nosy old man asking idiotic questions.

'Evening, Master Percy,' I answered politely. Aunt Clara would have whooped me hard otherwise. 'I got to go and help Aunt Clara.' I hurried past him without looking at him and ran up the wooden stairs leading to the porch. The warm smell of baking filled my nose as soon as I entered the door, and despite my fears I suddenly felt hungry. I nearly forgot my mission as I tucked into a thick slice of warm delicious sweet potato pudding. I washed it down with Aunt Clara's egg punch, which is made up of a raw egg mixed with milk, sweetened with condensed milk and flavoured with vanilla and nutmeg. Ummm, you have to taste it to believe anything can taste that good, trust me!

After I showered in the lukewarm water from the tank and dressed in my yellow cotton pyjamas hand-stitched by Aunt Clara, I picked up the well-used family Bible and sat by Aunt Clara's feet to begin my nightly read. I read Psalm 91, the psalm of protection. Aunt Clara read it every day and she always read it aloud when she was troubled or sad or if there was someone or something trying to harm her. These someones or some-things were usually '*duppies*' (ghosts) or 'bad-minded people', people who would want to see harm come to you. I finished my recital, put the Bible back in its special place, a small table in the corner of the room, and laid it open on Psalm 91 as I had found it.

Though Aunt Clara was an old lady she wasn't too old to know when something was on my mind.

'Come and sit side of yuh old aunt and tell me what yuh're considering so hard.' She patted the floor with her right foot.

I walked slowly and knelt before her, resting my hand on her knee.

'Aunt Clara . . . I can't go to London-Foreign,' I said quickly.

'Why?'

'It no nice there . . . it . . . it's a whole heap further

205

than twelve acres . . . the people . . . ice drop outta the
sky . . . yuh have to wear ten sweaters . . . if a whitey
look 'pon me I'll die,' I finished desperately and I knew
I didn't make much sense.

Aunt Clara's long drawn-out laugh filled the house.
She put a hand on her raised stomach and laughed even
more. She doubled over on the chair and laughed. In
fact, she was laughing so much, tears came streaming
down her black shiny face and she had to use the apron
tied around her large waist to wipe them away. For the
next ten minutes I watched helplessly as Aunt Clara
doubled over with laughter, hugging me and laughing
until I began to laugh too.

Eventually she was able to stop laughing. She pulled
me into her soft meaty arms and hugged me tightly.

'I'm scared, Aunt Clara, I don't want to go . . .'

'Shhhhhhhhh, nothing to be scared of honey-child,
nothing to be scared of.'

'But it's so far, it's a long way across the sky, Aunt
Clara.'

'Yes, but it's not the end of the earth – yuh can come
visit me in yuh holidays.'

'I don't want to go, I not going,' I said, as stubborn as
I could.

'It's a good opportunity for yuh. Yuh'll go to a good
school and get good hospital treatment if yuh get sick
and yuh can go visit Big Ben and the queen. Don't
yuh want to see the great tower? Go on one of them
two-storey buses?'

'Kelly says her ma says . . .'

'Kelly hasn't got much more common sense than her

ma, and her ma has none. They don't know nothing so don't go letting them scare yuh. Stand up for me.' Aunt Clara held my hands at arm's length, looking up and smiling proudly at me. 'Yuh've grown to be a fine woman and I will miss yuh, but I need yuh to go to this foreign place and learn new things and meet different people then yuh come back home and teach yuh Aunt Clara all about it.'

'It'll be lonely.'

'It'll be magical – yuh'll have yuh likkle brother to look forward to meeting, and then there's yuh ma and yuh new pa.'

I withdrew my hands roughly, hiding them behind my back. I stared accusingly at Aunt Clara who simply smiled gently back at me.

'Even if yuh were my own chile I would want yuh to go to London. It's good for yuh, Justice, it's good and it's educational.'

'Oh, Aunt Clara!' I threw my arms around her neck and sobbed. 'Please, please, please don't make me, don't make me go, I'll die over there, they'll kill me.'

Aunt Clara chuckled again. 'Shhhhhhhh, come on now, dry them tears and I'll make yuh a promise.'

I used my pyjama sleeves to wipe my eyes and nose. Sniffing, I asked, 'What promise?'

Aunt Clara's warm chubby hands cupped my face and she used her thumbs to wipe away the tracks left by my tears.

'Yuh is my world, Justice. Ever since yuh ma left yuh with me when yuh were six weeks old. I love yuh; I want the best for yuh. I want yuh to go to Foreign and come back educated so yuh can make a good life. I don't want yuh to live all yuh life in this one-room house. It's all right for me but there's much more out there for yuh and it's time to get it. Yuh next birthday yuh're a teenager – and if by then yuh don't like Foreign, I'll come and take yuh home with me.'

'Really?' I suddenly felt hope again.

'It's my word.'

I promised Aunt Clara that I wouldn't cry, but even as I made that promise I knew I was lying because as soon as I was on that plane I fully intended to cry as loud as I possibly could so that they would send me home. And I really, really wanted to cry, and would have cried – if I had remembered that I wanted to cry. The excitement of actually flying on Air Jamaica! I was in a plane and it didn't even feel as if it were moving, but I could see the clouds below and could hardly believe that I was actually flying in the sky above them. I fell asleep happy; my belly full to the brim with the *ackee* and salt fish meal dished out on the plane and the fruit punch. It was only the jolt of the plane as it landed that eventually woke me up. The captain's voice came out of the loud-speaker, welcoming everyone to London but asking them to remain in their seats with seat belts intact until told otherwise. As if anybody was listening to him. Everyone was getting up and reaching for their hand luggage to get off the plane, but I was a minor travelling alone and had to wait for one of them air hostesses to accompany me to my mother – that's what they said anyway.

I had only ever seen a picture of my mother. It sat in a silver frame on Aunt Clara's bookshelf, along with pictures of other family members, some of them long dead. I was unprepared for how young she would look, dressed in tight jeans and a white shirt, her hair in braids with purple beads, which also matched her lipstick and her nails. Her arms felt strange when they hugged me, she didn't have a big soft body like Aunt Clara, but she sure smelt good – all fresh like Aunt Clara's flower garden after it rained. I watched quietly as she twirled me around, telling me how tall and beautiful I was, and when she said I looked like my father, all I wanted to do was ask her who he was. But I didn't. Aunt Clara told me how he broke her heart and wouldn't believe I was his child, something to do with my light brown skin and soft wavy hair. He was a dark-skinned man and even though my mother was half Chinese and half black, he couldn't see why the child, me, had to come out like 'some white pickaninny'. I don't care; I don't need him.

Kelly was wrong. London wasn't so cold. It was September and I only needed one sweater. My mum said it wouldn't get cold until November. I liked my new house. I liked Jackie too, my little brother. I had a room to myself and it was big, real big, and get this: I had a television, video, DVD and a hi-fi set, and it had a CD! I wasn't too sure how to work them at first, but Jackie had fun teaching me and laughing at what I didn't know, and that was a whole lot of laughing. Jack was cool. He was my new dad. He's white with a bushy ginger beard around his pink round face and none on

head. He said I could call him Jack but Aunt Clara
would have whooped me proper if she had ever heard
me calling an adult by their first name. So I called him
Mr Jack and he laughed and said I should call him
Uncle Jack instead. He took me around London in his
black taxi. He drove me and Jackie around like royalty
and pointed out Buckingham Palace and Big Ben. I
wished I had kept the dream of them in my head
because they weren't as magical as I thought. Jackie
introduced me to Fish and Chips and Pizzas and I loved
them! Aunt Clara would drop dead at the thought of
me eating from complete strangers! Oh, Kelly was so
wrong and I laughed at myself for believing all her scare
stories. I look in Uncle Jack's face every day and I ain't
dropped dead yet. I wrote and told Aunt Clara and it
gave me the greatest pleasure to tell Kelly.

School was another story. Don't get me wrong, I liked
it but it was different from St Helen's in Jamaica. The
kids were so rude to the teachers; I could hardly believe
my ears at the language they used in the classrooms.
Cuss words were in every sentence for some kids,
whether they were talking to their friends or a teacher.
One day Sarah Harley, a girl in my class, attacked Miss
Hunt, thumped her in her face, and blood came pouring out of her nose. That never happened at St Helen's
or any school I knew in Jamaica. The teachers would
have whooped you real bad!

They had gangs too and rules, stupid rules, which
I didn't pay no mind. Like once two black girls in my
class approached me and told me that I was dissing. I

asked them how and one told me that I was talking to the 'greys'. Well, I asked what that was and they laughed at me. 'White people,' they said, walking off still laughing.

Then Belinda Simms, this big fat black girl, had the cheek to ask me if I was mixed. She said my skin was fair and though I got nigger in my hair, it wasn't a hundred per cent nigger so I shouldn't talk to anyone in her gang as they were black, excuse me! I asked Sylvia Peters what 'mixed' was and she said it was when one parent is black and the other white, Indian, Chinese or any mixture. Who really cares?

'If you're mixed,' Sylvia informed me, 'you can be accepted as black if you can prove how black you are.'

Well, I told her it made no sense to me and walked off.

Soon they, the different gangs, realized that I didn't follow their rules. I talked to who I wanted to talk to, as long as they talked back to me. The black girls, or 'The Bling Tings' as they were known, watched me hard and I knew they wanted to say something to me but they thought I was a Yardie. With me just coming from Jamaica they seemed to somehow respect the reputation, though they didn't love it.

I acquired a strange new friend, Maya Knowles, and she was white. Well, it was more Maya adopting me than me acquiring her. It seemed as if she was every gang's punchbag, the whites as much as the blacks and Indians targeted her, especially after PE in the showers where the teacher never entered. They would push her around and throw her clothes in the showers, punch and kick her; it was unbearable to watch and I would often get out of there as quickly as possible. Until the day when the white girl gang held her naked on the floor and were actually going to use a broom on her, with all the other gangs laughing and cheering them on. Not in front of me, not any more, Aunt Clara would have shaken her head in disappointment if I hadn't helped. So I did. I pushed my way into the centre of the circle where they had her and pushed them all off, one by one. I helped Maya up from the cold floor and put a towel around her. She was shaking and crying so badly and I was feeling so disgusted with myself for taking so long to help her that I was willing to smash all their faces to a pulp. And I would have been willing to take them all on. I told Maya to go and get dressed.

The circle fell apart, giving way to us. Cold steely eyes from young pretty faces, plain faces, faces with pimples, all different shades and colours glared at us. I was pretty scared, but only inside; outside I glared back at the sea of faces, daring who dared to come and test.

The next morning Maya came up to me and held out a pretty crisp twenty-pound note. 'For helping me,' she announced. I didn't want to take it but she insisted and wouldn't take no for an answer, so I took it to make her happy – honest!

At lunch break Sylvia Peters asked me if I hadn't heard about Stephen Lawrence.

'Which class is he in?' I asked her.

'He's dead,' she said. 'Killed by Nazis.'

'Germans?' I asked. I'd heard all about them on the World Service, something about World War Two, but that happened years ago. She laughed and explained how a black teenage boy, Stephen Lawrence, was murdered by a gang at a bus stop, but no one went to prison for it. It was only then that I realized how pretty she was. She explained who the Nazis were, and how there were white people like them still around. I didn't say nothing, I thought about Uncle Jack and how kind and funny he was and how he made me feel just as loved as Aunt Clara. He wasn't a Nazi.

'You've got to stop dissing the programme, Justice. Belinda is beginning to get pissed off.'

'Why can't I talk to who I want?'

'It's the way it is, Justice, and Belinda is stirring it with the other Bling girls.'

'That Belinda needs someone to teach her a lesson, and I just might be the one to do it.'

'It's for your own good, Justice. White people don't really like us you know. I know you ain't been here long, but don't you see who does all the dirty work in this country? Who are the ones always serving the master? It's us!' she said earnestly, and I knew she really believed what she said and maybe that was all she'd seen, but I had Uncle Jack and so I couldn't believe or see things the way she and the other Bling girls did.

'But your Bling girls beat up black girls, too. Sabrina beat up Ajoa just for having the same hairstyle as her,' I pointed out.

'Yeah, but Ajoa is *too* black. She comes from Africa – Uganda – monkey land.' She chuckled but I didn't laugh. I just looked at her in disgust and she looked away, embarrassed.

From my first day at the school I had been trying to understand London ways, but I was getting tired of the threat that always seemed to be hanging around me like a shadow — I always had to watch my back. Kelly was right there, but it was more from the black girls than the white.

Uncle Jack could drive you anywhere in London, he knew every street and alley, but if you wanted help with your homework you wouldn't go to Jack. Yet his wisdom often reminded me of Aunt Clara. He would say stuff that made sense, make you think or rethink, so I told him about the different posses at school and the problems, and how they thought I was a traitor. He rubbed his ginger beard and looked thoughtful.

'What people think about you don't have to become your business. Often times when you stand up to the bullies, they sit down. You have a wonderful name; I think it means you'll do the right thing.'

I waited for more, but that was it. I was disappointed but I didn't say nothing.

Sylvia met me at the school gate the next morning, looking at me all odd.

'Belinda's in care, lucky sod. Her mum hit her for coming home at three a.m. and she called the police and had her locked up. Now she's in a foster home.'

'Locked up her mother? She's the one who should

be locked up. What she doing out at three a.m.? Aunt Clara would whoop me good.'

'Well, this country ain't like Jamaica. Adults can't mess with us, we just call Childline and get them locked up.'

Now I was really disgusted and Sylvia saw it and attempted to change my opinions.

'You know how much money and freedom you get in care? You can buy new trainers and clothes every month!' She looked at me as if I was crazy not to agree.

'Anyway, Belinda's safe but you're not. They found out that your stepdad's white.'

I froze. Knowing how they were I hadn't never told no one about Uncle Jack, or that my little brother Jackie was mixed. Not that I was ashamed or scared, I just didn't want no problems.

News travels fast in the corridors of a school, in the toilets, the playground and even in the library. The news was that Belinda, along with a few of her Bling Tings, was going to jump me after school for having a white stepdad. Maya met me at lunchtime and told me she'd walk home with me.

'I can't fight but I take long before I really hurt. I can take their beatings and it'll give you time to fight Belinda.'

I felt a lump in my throat. I realized I wanted to cry. Her kind offer made me know for sure that the stupid law of sticking to your own racial group was really dumb. She gave me a strange feeling of courage and I hugged her.

Sylvia slipped me a note telling me to pretend sick so that I could leave school before Belinda, but I knew it would only mean facing the whole thing again another day, and I was anxious to get it out of the way.

I walked by myself after school. I saw the crowd gathering for the fight outside the gates. I thought about running, then I thought about Uncle Jack and Maya and I felt strength coming from somewhere. They opened the circle to let me in, and I saw Belinda and two of the Bling girls. I had expected more. I looked at them, trying to look hard and mean, and I threw my bag to one side and kicked off my shoes. The two girls looked scared and Belinda startled. I tucked my skirt into the elasticized legs of my knickers and took a step towards them. The two girls ran and it was my turn to look startled. They struggled through the crowd, shouting that it was Belinda's idea and they didn't really want to fight me.

I felt encouraged by this, and took a step to face Belinda. She was a bigger build than me, but I was taller, so I was kind of looking down at her.

'Let me get this right,' I told her, pointing my index finger in her face without touching her. 'You want to fight me because my stepdad is white? Because I look mixed? Because I talk to everyone? Can you tell me what's wrong with all that?' I was still scared, but I was madder.

It went really quiet and everyone had their eyes on Belinda, waiting to hear her answers. Guess what? She had none. I thought it would be the perfect time to let everyone know a few more things about me.

'I ain't having you fools,' I shout at her and then at the crowd, 'telling me who I can talk to.' They all seemed to be waiting for my next words, including Belinda, and I felt like I was being worshipped. I circled Belinda with both hands on my hips, looking her up and down, then looking at the crowd. 'I'll talk to black, white, Chinese, Japanese and any nese I want and it's none of my business what any of you think about that.' I heard the crowd sniggering. 'Now if you're ready to fight,' I rolled up my sleeves, 'I'll give you what you want and then I'll eat your liver raw.' I stood close to her face.

Shocked whispers were all around me. Belinda looked horrified. She was looking everywhere but at me and I knew I had won without having to lift a hand.

Mr Solomon, the science teacher, came rushing through, telling everyone to get off home or come inside for detention. I fixed my clothes, put my shoes back on and was about to pick up my bag when Sylvia handed it to me. She and Maya hugged me and the crowd started to cheer.

School has never been the same since. There was this new kind of respect for me coming from all the posses. Everyone wanted to say 'hi', smile or wave. Sylvia and especially Maya liked it because it meant everyone had the respect for them too.

I wrote and told Aunt Clara all about it and she wrote back asking all kind of questions about Belinda. She said Belinda wasn't bad, just sad, because no happy person goes around bullying people and I should try and find out what was bothering her.

I was horrified at Aunt Clara's suggestion; I didn't have a decent word to say to Bully Belinda. She was the school's tyrant for Christ's sake! But I couldn't help feeling sorry for her. She was no longer 'Top Bling' and her own posse avoided her, though not even that made a difference to her bullish ways. Then Maya started feeling sympathy pains for her too and said no one deserved to be cut off like that – not even Belinda. The way she said it you just knew she was remembering when everyone avoided her.

It wasn't easy, I tell you. But I did it. I spoke to her, by the bike shed where she hung out by herself at break times. She looked more miserable than mean, and scared when she saw me. She had a half-smoked cigarette between her fingers, but didn't look like she was enjoying it.

I stared at her, watched as she puffed and coughed on the cigarette until she got fed up of me just staring.

'Why're you staring at me?'

'What's wrong with hanging out with other races?' I went directly to the point.

She looked puzzled, then annoyed.

'That's a dumb question.'

'I'm asking it anyway.'

'Why're you talking to me? I don't even like you and I know you don't like me.'

'I don't really know you, so I can't say I don't like you.'

The words were just popping into my head from somewhere. Aunt Clara, I think.

'You want to come round my house? Meet my

Uncle Jack and my mum and brother? Uncle Jack's real cool, he'll make you laugh.'

Her mouth fell open and she was shaking her head in disbelief.

'Sunday's a good day,' I continued, ignoring the increasing look of scorn on her face.

'No it's not and I don't!' she shouted, but she looked confused, not mad. 'I don't know why you're doing this but I don't need to meet your sorry-punk family.'

'If you can't make Sunday, Uncle Jack says I can have a barbecue in two weeks, when school breaks for summer, so you can come to that instead if you like.'

I don't know why I kept the invite open, especially with her attitude, but once I'd had the opportunity of talking to Belinda on her own, I realized that she wasn't as bad as she'd like to think. Aunt Clara was right.

As the holidays approached, my coming barbecue was the talk of the school and it was near impossible trying to keep to twenty people like Mum and Uncle Jack said, especially when the whole of Year Eight expected an invitation.

I started to notice that every time I turned around, Belinda wasn't far away. I wasn't the only one who noticed. Sylvia said she saw Belinda looking at me in Assembly and then again in PE. She just looked though, and never said anything. Not until the last day of summer term that year. I can't remember exactly what she said, but two weeks later she was at my barbecue an hour before it finished to the surprise of everyone there.

We're now in Year Eleven preparing for our GCSEs and guess who's the school student mentor for race? Guess who chairs meetings on race relations in our school? Guess who won the award for Champion for Race in our school last year?

My best friend Belinda!

Rasheda Ashanti Malcolm was born in Jamaica and came to Britain as a young child. She has a degree in Media Studies and an MA in Creative and Transactional Writing from Brunel University. Her first attempt at a novel won her a weekend writing holiday. She went on to edit the black women's lifestyle magazine Candace *and currently teaches creative writing. She lives in London and has four sons.*

The Returnee

by Chu-Ching Chen

A story set in modern-day Japan

I opened the heavy metal door of our flat and the morning sun gushed into the entrance. I turned back. Mother stood at the porch bathed in the orange sunlight, and I felt an urge to hug her. But I checked myself, realizing that such behaviour was no longer expected from me, a big girl of sixteen.

Instead, I asked her to repeat 'passport' and 'nothing to declare' for me once more. As she repeated those Japanese words, radiance overflowed from her face as though she were trying to outshine the sun.

I told her to come back soon. 'Daddy and I won't last long without you,' I said. She just looked at me, quizzically. Someone had turned off the light in her face. When I read in her eyes that she was repeating the very same line to me, *Daddy and I won't last long without you*, I lowered my eyes and hurried out of the flat. At the bottom of the building I glanced up. Mother had come out of the flat and was gazing down at me from the railings.

The first 'motherless' day went by just like any other day. I hardly talked to anybody at school, and hardly anybody talked to me. Nothing much happened, and I never expected anything to. Well, nothing happened except for this new girl who had just been transferred to our class. Her name was Hanae, and her family had just moved to our area – *this* area where I lived, anyway. I watched her pale complexion and her crease-less school uniform as she shyly introduced herself in front of the class, and decided she was no different from all the others in Saginomiya Girls' High School: rather smart, from an OK family, at any rate OKer than mine, with enough time and money to allow her to muse over where to get the latest version of *tamagochi* or that tartan dress with an above-knee hemline advertised in *Seventeen*. Our teacher told her to sit next to me, since that seat was vacant. But I knew full well she was just one of *them*. She'd have nothing to do with me, nor I with her.

Sometimes I wondered what on earth I was doing here in Saginomiya Girls' High School, among girls with whom I had nothing in common. Sometimes I wondered what I was doing here in Japan. Father had made Japan sound like paradise before he'd brought us here: clean streets, polite people, hundreds of ice cream flavours to choose from, thousands of cartoons and gadgets to occupy myself with. Which were all true. But he hadn't told us what it would cost us all. He hadn't foreseen what would become of Mother and me.

Mother had gone back to China that morning, for a one-month 'holiday'. That was how she had phrased it when she'd asked me to book her flights online.

'A holiday?' I'd asked, my eyes searching the computer screen for the cheapest deal from Tokyo Narita to Beijing International.

'Yes, a holiday,' Mother had insisted. 'I know what you're thinking: "From *what*, Mum? You don't even work." Well, let me tell you this: just being here, just being in Japan, is hard work for me. I need a holiday just from being in this country.'

I needed a holiday, too. But I couldn't leave just like that. I had school to attend, and since Mother wouldn't be here for a month, I took it for granted that I should take over her job of pouring my father that nightly mug of daisy tea when he got home, and topping it up with lots and lots of water.

That evening when I finished my homework, I stood up from my desk and paced to the window. The straw-woven *tatami* mats felt soft, but a bit cool under my feet. They mildly reflected the light from the lamp in the middle of my room and emitted a pale yellowish shimmer. I rested my elbows on the window sill, then my chin in my palms. My bedroom window looked out diagonally on a building where, outside a window on the second floor, a red-and-yellow neon sign flashed: ALL LUCK COME – CHINESE RESTAURANT. That was where my father worked. Every quarter of an hour or so, I'd catch a glimpse of Father passing by that window, usually with something in his hand: a head of Chinese leaf, a wok. The beads of sweat on his forehead, the anxious look on his face, however, might be products of my imagination, since at this distance they were unlikely to be visible. And as for imagination, I had a wild one, wilder than I cared to admit to my parents.

Leaning on the window sill I wondered what 'souvenir' Father would bring me that night. For anything brought back from anywhere is called a souvenir in Japan: the little bags filled with lavender you bring back from France for your classmates, the box of *yatsuhashi* cakes you bring back from Kyoto for your friends at work, the rice crackers you bring home to your wife from the station kiosk. Come to think of it, it was only by that image of my father in the window frame across the street and the nightly souvenir that I was linked to him. There were no reminders of his presence otherwise. He usually came back home after I had long gone to bed; he'd be still fast asleep when I went to school in the morning. I'd go to bed knowing when I woke up in the morning, a souvenir would be waiting for me on the breakfast table. It was usually in the form of food: fried golden buns with a condensed milk dip, shrimp balls covered with fried breadcrumbs, steamed shrimp and cabbage dumplings with translucent wrappers. These were all made by the other chef – the Cantonese one. My father was the Northern chef; he worked on dishes like boiled, thick-wrapped dumplings, roast spring onion pancakes and red-stewed pork. I'd heat up my father's souvenirs in the microwave for breakfast. Satisfying breakfasts they always were: I relished that mild, often sweet Southern flavour, a change from the savoury though equally tasty dishes my parents made.

Occasionally Father brought me other things. Once it had been an embroidered Chinese knot, given to him by a customer. Those knots are supposed to bring you good luck. Another time he had brought home to me this intricately patterned black hairslide. It had stayed in the lost-and-found drawer for six months and the restaurant owner had wanted to get rid of it. I don't know if he smiled in relief or sneered in mockery when my father asked for his permission to take it home, but anyway the owner consented. At first glance I knew it was one of those hairslides I had drooled over in department stores, those that would cost 2,000 yen apiece and that I'd never had the heart to ask my parents to buy for me. For several months I clipped my hair with it almost every day. It remained my favourite.

I watched the red-and-yellow neon sign outside the restaurant flash and flash and I waited. I waited for my father to come home; I waited to pour him that mug of daisy tea. I also waited to ask him questions: what on earth we were doing here, so that he had to work such long hours, so that Mother had got so fed up she'd gone back home, so that I had to pretend to be someone I wasn't. When the flashing of red and yellow became boring, my eyes shifted focus: the outline of a young girl's face – my own reflection in the window – emerged from the building and the neon lights. To kill time I pretended to myself that I was only seeing this face for the first time, in the street for instance, and I examined it part by part to see if I could recognize anything un-Japanese. A simple bob, thick and shiny black hair, with an almost too neat fringe: Japanese enough. Eyebrows a bit too thick: un-Japanese. Eyes of an almond shape, very dark: Japanese enough. The nose having melted into the background, I could only see my round nostrils: neutral, neither Japanese nor un-Japanese. Full lips, corners tilted downwards as if sulking: un-Japanese. Overall, the face would be presumed Japanese until proven otherwise, but that made me feel all the more like a fraud. I told people everywhere I was Takeda Mariko: registering with the Ward Council, signing up for a video shop, ordering pizza over the phone. But the Zhou Chunhua in me, the Zhou Chunhua that had been my identity for the first fourteen years of my life, kept lurking around and asking, her head tilted, her voice quiet, 'What about me?' And Takeda Mariko would blush with guilt and shame.

The doorbell rang at twelve-thirty. Father looked tired on the doorstep. I offered him my arm, almost ushering him inside. I helped him sit down in a chair. It was only then that I noticed his hands were empty.

'Huar,' Father said, calling me by my Chinese nickname. He called me Huar and spoke Chinese with me inside the family; in front of Japanese people he'd call me Mariko and make painstaking efforts to express himself in Japanese. 'Huar,' he said, 'I learned a new word at All Luck Come today – oh, get me some tea first.'

I poured a mug of daisy tea for him: the dried daisies floated up and spread out as they got soaked.

I sat down, too. I watched Father sip his daisy tea loudly. He let out satisfied sighs between the sips, oblivious to the new word he had learned. I waited a few seconds, but sorting out why we were here seemed much more urgent than helping Father with another Japanese word he'd come across. Memories of the colourless days at school surged to my mind, and I blurted out, 'Dad, why have you brought Mum and me to Japan?'

Father stopped short. He was holding the mug close to his mouth, looking down at the tea, rounding his lips for another sip, but his hand and his lips froze at my question. Only his eyelids, wrinkled and triangular with age, flipped up. 'What was that?'

Uneasily I repeated my question.

Father thumped the mug on the table, stood up and towered over me. 'Why have I brought you to Japan? Have I worked fifteen hours today just to come home and hear you ask me this?'

I crouched in my chair. I didn't dare to look at Father.

'I have returned to my own country! I'm Japanese! You and Mum are my family, so this is your country, too. That's why I've brought you here. Look at you. Look at your clothes. Look at your textbooks and note-books and pens. That's why I've brought you here. Look at the school you go to. That's why I've brought you here.'

'But I don't like that school. I have no friends . . .'

'Don't tell me that's my problem! I make sure I send you to that expensive girls' school, and you make sure

227

you like it! Do you think I have money burning in my pocket that I can't wait to get rid of? Don't you know sending you to that school means working an extra six hours a day for me?'

I kept my head low. I stared at my feet as I shuffled them. I tried to breathe as soundlessly as possible. Father stepped backwards and dropped himself in to the chair. He took up his mug again and put it to his lips.

I drew a deep breath and ventured, 'Is the tea cold, Dad? I'll top it up for you.'

He gazed at me, and sighed. He handed me the mug without saying a word. I topped it up with some more water from the thermos and handed the mug back to him. He nodded at me.

'Huar, haven't your classmates invited you to their houses?'

'They have, once or twice, but I . . . I . . . I turned them down. I've been to a café with them once, and I felt . . . I felt as if I were transparent, as if I were part of the air . . .'

'Talk sense,' Father interrupted me. I looked up and saw in his face both impatience and embarrassment.

'Huar, I was just going to tell you a new word I learned at All Luck Come today. Listen, from now on, everybody you meet, you tell them you're a *kikoku-shijo*. *Kikoku-shijo*, can you remember that?'

Father didn't speak much Japanese, and it was almost pitiable to see him labour on all the k's of that word. I nodded eagerly and reassured him, '*Kikoku-shijo*, yes, Dad, yes.'

He smiled. '*Kikoku-shijo*, you tell them that. They'll

invite you to their houses. And you must invite them home, too. I'll cook you a huge Chinese meal. You have to do that. Bring a friend home.'

Kikoku-shijo. So that was the souvenir he brought me tonight.

In the warmth of my futon and the darkness of my room, I chewed the word over and over in my mouth. *Kikoku-shijo* – a *returnee child*? Well, there was probably nothing against me saying I was a returnee child: I was half Japanese and my father had returned to his own country from China. But in my heart I knew too well that when one thought of a *kikoku-shijo*, one had in one's mind a girl with fair complexion – possibly the result of having lived in a colder climate – or a boy who chewed gum and, instead of walking, 'skateboarded'; a Japanese child whose father had worked in America or France or Germany and had taken his family along; a youth who spoke perfect English or French or some other posh language, who dressed and behaved differently. Not someone like me. *Kikoku-shijo*s didn't return from countries like China, they didn't speak non-Western foreign languages and they weren't half-bred.

We had moved from China to Japan two years before. Father had ended up in north-eastern China because his parents, originally farmers in Sado County, Niigata Prefecture, Japan, had gone over there during World War Two. The area was Japan's colony then, and my grandparents went there after several years of poor harvests in Sado County, in search of a better life.

However, the life of these 'Pioneers', as they were called by the Japanese government, hardly improved. As Japan was losing the war in 1945, three-quarters of the colony was abandoned with its defenceless citizens. The Soviet Union's attack on the colony in August that year resulted in many deaths of the Pioneers, many separations of families and many 'wartime orphans'. Father never told me what exactly had happened then or how my grandparents had died; all I knew was that he, too, had become a wartime orphan in the summer of 1945.

Like most other wartime orphans, my father was adopted by a local Chinese family, given a Chinese name and raised as their own child. Like most other orphans, he forgot his mother tongue completely. He even forgot his Japanese name except for the first character. He grew up as a Chinese, married a Chinese woman, started a Chinese family. The wartime orphans like my father would have lived on like that all their lives, if they hadn't been given an opportunity some forty years later to visit Japan to find their own parents. After countless phone calls and endless paperwork, one day it happened: I tagged along behind my parents and got myself transported to Tokyo. With the help of some relatives we settled down in Nakano Ward. However, our relatives had a hard time communicating with us; besides, they were more or less dispersed in the country. So there we were, the Zhous changed overnight into the Takedas, very much on our own, lost in the jungle of a big city.

No, I wasn't a proper *kikoku-shijo*, no matter how I

looked at it. Nevertheless, I was willing to be obedient and tell people I was one. For one thing, that would make up for the occasional slip of the tongue I committed when speaking Japanese. Besides, I wouldn't mind having a friend – if saying I was a returnee to satisfy my father could really win me one – to keep for myself.

The next morning, as I was eating breakfast alone in the kitchen, I wondered how I could go about telling people I was a *kikoku-shijo*. I couldn't knock on my classmates' doors and have them out on their doorsteps to hear me declare I was a returnee. I'd have to tell new people I met and then let the word spread. Suddenly a face crossed my mind like a light switched on: that of our new classmate, Hanae.

All day in class I glanced sideways at Hanae sitting next to me and wondered how I could manage to engage her in a chat and bring out the issue of who I was. During the first couple of breaks I hadn't any chance to talk to her: our classmates surrounded her and bombarded her with questions. Hanae smiled at all of them. She had a disarming smile. I sensed that Hanae was going to blend well with them, much better than I did. During the last break, however, nobody came over, because the next class was PE, and everyone was getting gym shoes out of their rucksacks and putting on their jerseys. While Hanae and I were doing the same, we started exchanging a few words. Hanae asked me what my name was, where I lived. I answered and asked her a question or two. Then she said, 'Did you come from another part of Japan, just like me? There are a couple of words that you pronounce the . . . the Kansai way . . . or is it Shikoku . . .?'

I cleared my throat but no words came out. My heart was beating away maniacally. All the blood in my body dashed to my neck and cheeks. I cleared my throat once more.

'Well, actually, I'm a *kikoku-shijo*.'

I could hardly bring myself to look at her.

'Oh, where from?' Admiration registered in her voice. 'So do you perhaps speak better English than Japanese?'

I felt my cheeks were so heated they could explode.

'We . . . we lived in –'

At that point the bell rang. As we hurried out of the classroom Hanae said, 'Let me hear how you speak English one day.' And I felt as though I had told a huge lie.

I was in a good mood as I approached school the next day. It was a crisp April morning, a bit chilly, but pleasantly so, and you could hear a few birds chirping in the trees around the schoolyard. Along the road in front of our school, cherry trees were just beginning to blossom, tiny buds of a near-white, elegant pink colour opening up shyly from the dark boughs.

A few of my classmates were chatting and giggling under a gingko tree in one corner of the schoolyard. Seeing Hanae was also there, I went towards them. But I couldn't help noticing that while the other girls were red and purple with agitation, Hanae had a quizzical expression on her face.

One of them saw me and cried out, 'Hey, here she

is!' – a response I hadn't expected and didn't understand. The other girls all turned to me, their mouths and eyes wide open, and then laughed out loud.

'Oh yes, here she is! Here's the *kikoku-shijo*, the *returnee*!'

'A returnee whose father doesn't even speak proper Japanese!'

'And yet her father's twice as much Japanese as she is!'

My heart stopped beating right there and then. My feet stopped advancing, too. So there I was, at this ridiculous distance from the girls, close enough to communicate verbally, but far enough to let anybody make out I was excluded.

I was silent, that was clear. But I had become deaf, too. I could see the girls making funny faces and shouting and giggling, but I couldn't hear the sounds they were making any more. I stood there, not feeling particularly uncomfortable, just numb. It struck me that this was very much my situation in school, and in Japan for that matter – my Japanese, my manners, my knowledge of the culture were all sufficient for me to communicate with any Japanese person, but still I was excluded from something in the core of the circle the girls formed, something I couldn't pinpoint. There was this invisible line between these girls and me, and I suppose as I was about to step on it, something punched me to ward me off.

In the soundless picture of agitation and movement, Hanae's face was fixed constantly towards me, watching me, apologetic, puzzled, concerned.

★

All day long I sat in class, staring blankly at the teacher, who seemed to change into another person each hour. I heard nothing. I really must have gone deaf. I just felt this heat boiling up from my navel, burning my whole torso, burning my neck and face. It was shame, and anger, anger at others and at myself. It was a burning reproach that I had shamed myself, my father and mother, and my country − yes, my country, my motherland China.

All the other girls appeared to have forgotten about what had happened, except for Hanae, who shot me quick glances all day long, always in the moments between looking up from her notebook and fixing her eyes on the teacher.

After school, as I was putting away textbooks and notebooks into my rucksack, Hanae approached me. 'Mariko-chan . . .' She sounded tentative. 'I'd really like to hear your family's experiences in . . . I'd really like to hear your experiences . . . abroad. My history teacher in my last school told us a bit about that part of history, and I never thought I'd actually meet somebody with that background.' She bit her lip. 'May I go to your house . . . and meet your parents?'

I nodded and lowered my head. I made myself busy moving the books around in my rucksack, rearranging their order. Did she see in me a potential friend or a potential sample of history? Was she being friendly to me or was she keen on getting a high mark? Whichever it was, I could finally bring a classmate home and get this task my father had given me out of the way.

★

That night at twelve-thirty, I told Father a new friend I'd made at school would like to visit us. I did this when opening the souvenir pack he had brought me. I had already handed him the mug of daisy tea.

'Oh,' he said, 'oh.' He rubbed his rough but warm palms together, and just kept saying, 'Oh.'

The souvenir he'd brought me that night was half a dozen steamed shrimp dumplings: red shrimps showing inside translucent crescents of wrappers.

'When is she coming? Do you think she'd fancy Chinese dumplings? What sort of filling, Chinese leaf and pork or spring chives and eggs? What do you reckon?'

Father nodded ardently as I gave him some vague answers, but I suspected he wasn't really listening.

'Huar, did you . . . did you tell this new friend of yours that you were a *kikoku-shijo*?' Father asked, like a teacher summoning his favourite pupil to answer a difficult question.

'Yes, I did. She's new in our class so when she asked about us, I told her.'

Father let out a nervous laugh, and rubbed his large palms more vigorously than ever. 'I told you, you see, I told you.'

As Hanae sat down to the feast at Sunday noon, I could see she was stunned. Five plates of Chinese dumplings were lying on the table, giving off steam and lustre. They were so full some looked as if they were going to burst. The edges were beautifully gathered, and curiously, although somewhat deformed by the boiling, they looked all the more tempting. They lay there like a hundred laughing mouths, or a hundred careless, well-fed bellies, waiting for chopsticks to pick them up and pop them into watering mouths.

Father had asked to take half a day off and had been cooking all morning.

'Wow, I've never even *seen* so many dumplings in my life, Mr Takeda!' Hanae exclaimed, swallowing saliva.

Hanae was wearing a light pink jumper and a matching cardigan, navy-blue skirt, and flat-heeled black shoes. It was the first time I saw her in anything other than the school uniform. Set off by her jumper and cardigan, her cheeks looked pink, too. I watched her and wondered if this girl had known any misery in her life.

Father obviously took Hanae's remark as a compliment, and his whole face was sweetly wrinkled up with contentment. He picked up a couple of dumplings with his chopsticks and dropped them into Hanae's plate. 'Eat, eat.' His warm hospitality masked his infantile Japanese.

'Dad?' I took a stealthy glance at Hanae. 'Let Hanae-chan help herself.'

'All right, all right, help yourself, Hanae-san.' Father took a dumpling for himself and started eating.

As the meal progressed, Father became more and more talkative. It was partly the *sake* he was sipping, of course, but I could tell it was also Hanae, or the fact that I had brought her home, that she was sitting here in the kitchen with us.

Hanae ate slowly, savouring each bit of food she had in her mouth. She kept telling Father how delicious his dumplings were.

Father was proud. 'Oh, Hanae-san, I lived in north-east China. In north-east China, dumpling delicious, but also many other foods delicious. I cook you more in future.'

'Mr Takeda, Mariko-chan told me about how your family got to north-eastern China. I've heard a bit about what happened during the war, and I'd really like to know more. Could I ask you some questions after this feast? I'm actually thinking of writing my history term paper on it, that is, if I collect enough information.'

Hanae said all this amiably. Still, I wasn't sure if I liked what she said.

Father, however, didn't seem to mind. 'Oh, no need wait till after meal, ask me now. Mariko never ask me. I wish she ask me.'

I glared at him. 'You've never wanted me to know anything, Dad.'

Father ignored me. He belched and said, 'Hanae-san, ask, ask.'

'Well, Mr Takeda, could you tell me what exactly happened when Japan surrendered in 1945?'

'Oh, I remember clear, Hanae-san. We living in Dong'an Province at the time. It was 27 August, I remember clear. Japan have already surrender, but we not yet know.'

I didn't know what we were in for, but I immediately sensed whatever Father had to say, it wasn't something I'd like Hanae to hear.

'So what happened on that day?' Hanae was all ears.

Father took one more sip of his *sake*, slurped and gurgled.

'Since morning Mother tell me never go outside. Around eleven-thirty we hear sound like thunder, it shake all our window glass off. The Soviets fired a cannon ball. They want to crack open our village gate. Mother hold my baby sister and me tight. I become afraid Soviet soldiers just come in and shoot us all. When Mother looking after baby sister, I get me free and rush out of our house.

'The village is full with Pioneers, lots of women and kids. I see young man in army uniform, maybe nineteen or twenty, and a few women around him. They all shouting and screaming, "Quick, please, kill me, kill me!" The soldier hold up pistol and shoot two youngest women. Then he look up the sky and shout, husky voice, "Long live His Majesty!" and shoot himself in the heart.'

I had put down my chopsticks. A half-eaten dumpling got stuck in my throat, refusing to go up or down. I stole a glance at Hanae. She was completely frozen. Her jaw hung loose and her eyes were fixed on my father's face as if tethered there by an invisible thread. Her chopsticks had stopped in mid-air, who knows for how long.

Father took no notice of us at all.

'At noon Soviet soldiers enter our village. They point guns here and there and shoot. I run to body of young soldier, young soldier just killed himself, and hide under his body. A few seconds and my face all covered by warm blood. My shirt also soaked by blood. A Soviet soldier come towards me. I hold breath. Slash! He slit my shirt with his bayonet. I know I'm killed.

'When I awake again, already evening. I see every house in our village burning. I lie still, I watch. Fifty metre from me, Soviet soldiers have builded a fire, they killing horses, roasting horsemeat, singing, laughing, drinking, dancing. Then it begin to fall tiny rain. It fall rain a long, long time.'

Father fell into silence. I ventured, careful not to break his trance, 'So what became of Grandpa and Grandma?'

Father's voice was calm. 'Grandpa, out since morning with other men and boys, don't know how he dead, but can imagine. Grandma, lived that day, hold baby sister in arms, hide in pigsty. Then went to asylum in Shenyang, yes, big city nearby. Baby dead on the way. Mother bury her in *kaoliang* [sorghum] field. In asylum no good food, no enough either. Died that winter. No even see next spring. I find out in Sado County record.'

I was speechless. I couldn't think of anything else to say.

'What was it like for you spending such a large part of your life in China?' Hanae asked gently.

Her question alerted me. Why hadn't I ever thought of that before? Despite all that I'd been told, my unconsciousness had made stubborn assumptions – that just like me, Father had never been anybody other than a 'North-easterner'; that just like me, Father had never had any other home than north-eastern China.

Obviously Hanae didn't see Father that way.

'Oh, Hanae-san, you ask that question, I'm happy, I'm happy. First, everything difficult. The other kids call me Japanese devil, they make fun of me, how I sit, how I walk, how I talk Chinese weird. Now I talk Japanese weird!' Father laughed heartily. 'But everything soon OK, very soon OK. I become Chinese and everyone think me Chinese.' Father looked at me. 'So I know Mariko will soon OK, very soon OK.'

For some reason I blushed.

Father took another sip of his *sake*. 'But in Cultural Revolution, people no think me Chinese any more. They remember I'm Japanese.'

'Uh . . .' Hanae frowned and turned to me. 'I've vaguely heard the name . . . but what exactly was the Cultural Revolution?'

'It was a political campaign started by the leader of China at the time. A large part of traditional culture was destroyed. It lasted ten years.' I told Hanae what I knew.

'Oh, Cultural Revolution, crazy time, everything upside down, everybody crazy,' Father said. 'Chinese fight Chinese, many people dead. But if you foreign, you even more bad. Foreign mean bad. They make me kneel on a wood board, a board for washing clothes, so there are many grooves. I kneel on it and my knees hurt and hurt. They hang a heavy placard from my neck, it say "Japanese devil". My neck hurt, my back hurt, my knees hurt. The call me names, all kinds of names, for several hours a time. They do these thing to fellow Chinese, too. They do these thing for no reason.

They make up reason. They say this man is spy, that woman is counter-revolutionary. In my case, they say this man is Japanese. And that make enough.'

I'm not sure how the rest of the afternoon passed by. I remember vaguely clearing the table. Perhaps we even had tea, I don't know. Again and again in my mind I went over the scenes my father had just described. And scenes I'd made up myself. How my grandmother had trembled all night in the pigsty where she hid with other Pioneers, how she wanted to find her family, dead or alive, the next morning, facing mountains of dead bodies and streams of blood. How my father's foster parents found this blood-covered boy, hungry and horrified. How they took him home and washed him, fed him, put him to bed. How my father knelt on the washboard and how the grooves ate into his flesh. How the placard, and possibly people's fists, kept his neck and back bent for hours and hours.

As I was showing Hanae out of our flat, my father's face became all wrinkled up again with a smile. 'Hanae-san, do come play with Mariko again. I make Chinese dumpling again.' But I was pretty sure this was the last I'd see Hanae in our home.

I accompanied her to the bus stop and said goodbye. When I returned to our flat, Father had already gone back to work.

That night, leaning on my window sill and staring at that window frame in which my father appeared from time to time, I felt envy for Hanae. I envied her for having asked the questions I myself should have asked.

For a brief moment, she had taken my place as my father's daughter.

At twelve-thirty Father returned to our flat. He handed me a packet of gold-and-silver buns; I handed him a mug of daisy tea. I watched his face for a while. He looked tired as usual, but not in the least unhappy.

'Dad,' I said almost inaudibly, 'I never knew you actually felt . . . Japanese.' My face burned. Illogically enough, it seemed something shameful to me for Father to have 'felt Japanese' in China.

I'd never seen Father's eyes so peaceful and forgiving. 'Oh, Huar, it was my home, of course, I miss it, I miss it. But . . . it was never quite my home. Now I've come to my own country. But this is never quite my home, either.' He paused. 'I know this isn't your mother's home, either. But I want it to be *your* home.'

At that moment something grasped me. I didn't know what it was – courage, perhaps, or bluntness, but probably more than anything else, trust.

I told Father, word by word, as clearly as I could, how it felt for me to be in Saginomiya Girls' High School, and how it felt for me to be in Japan. I told him it wasn't all peaches and cream as he supposed. For the first time, I trusted he'd understand.

Father listened in a way he never had. 'I see . . .' he said when I'd finished. 'I didn't realize all that, Huar. But . . . well, you see, I became Chinese. I was Chinese for many years. In the same way, you can become Japanese. I know you can.' He seemed lost in reverie. Supporting himself with one hand on the table he stood up, stepped forwards and looked into my eyes.

He patted the back of my head, then stroked my hair. He hadn't done so since I was a little girl, and the movements of his hand were as brief as they were imperceptible. He took his hand away and almost smiled. Then he turned and slowly shuffled to his bedroom.

That night I dreamt of Mother. I dreamt I was together with her in my grandparents' home in China; in my dream she smiled all the time.

On Monday morning Hanae called out my name from behind, outside our schoolyard. She caught up with me and flashed me that warm smile of hers and started chatting. She didn't thank me for the lunch the previous day; instead, she just started saying silly and sweet nothings, as if our friendship was already beyond unnecessary formality.

The cherry trees on both sides of the street were in full bloom now. For a few moments we walked in the tunnel of cherry blossoms in silence.

Then out of the blue, Hanae turned to me and said, 'Mariko-chan, I admire your father. I really do.' She grew a bit pensive. 'I've decided to write my history term paper on something else. But I'd love to go to your home again. I'd love to talk to your dad again, and meet your mum, and . . . have more Chinese food!' She laughed. 'And my mum says you must come over to our house and have a taste of everyday Japanese dishes, too.'

Before I realized it, I had already nodded at Hanae.

It was then we entered the school gate. Under the

same ginkgo tree in the schoolyard, our classmates were chatting away, eagerly catching up on their own week-end news. Some turned their heads our way and saw Hanae and me walking side by side. On their faces I saw surprise, confusion, indifference and, on one face, an attempt at a smile.

I looked at Hanae. She was smiling radiantly and – were my eyes deceiving me? – *proudly* at them.

All of a sudden, I didn't care any more. At each face I just smiled brightly. Whatever expression I saw, my response was the same.

Tonight I'll wait for Father again till he comes home at twelve-thirty, I thought. I'll sit him down and hand him a mug of daisy tea. I'll top it up with lots and lots of water. And I'll talk to him. I'll tell him I don't have to become Japanese. I'm Zhou Chunhua and I'm also Takeda Mariko. I have my childhood friends in China and I also have my friend Hanae in Japan. I'll tell Father that, when Mother comes back from China, the three of us, together with the friends I make, together with the friends they make, will find a way to survive, to flourish.

Side by side, Hanae and I walked towards the girls.

'Good morning,' Hanae and I said almost simultan-eously. It was a lovely April day, and for once, I truly wished every one of them a good morning.

Chu-Ching Chen (aka Li Jiang) is originally from Beijing, China. She likes to meet people from all over the world and deepen her understanding of different cultures, and she has a passion for languages. She obtained her honours and master's degrees in English literature at the University of Tokyo, Japan, and is currently completing her doctoral dissertation at the University of Nottingham, England.